BITTER Sweet

Nadia Marks was born in Cyprus, but grew up in North London, where she now lives with her husband and two sons. Formerly a creative director on a number of leading women's magazines, she now works as a freelance journalist for several national newspapers and magazines.

BITTER
Sweet

Nadia Marks

Piccadilly Press • London

First published in Great Britain in 2005
by Piccadilly Press Ltd,
5 Castle Road, London NW1 8PR

A catalogue record for this book is available from the British Library

ISBN: 1 85340 895 6 (trade paperback)

1 3 5 7 9 10 8 6 4 2

Printed and bound in Great Britain by Bookmarque Ltd
Typeset by Textype Typesetters
Cover design by Fielding Design
Set in Goudy

Papers used by Piccadilly Press are produced from forests grown and
managed as a renewable resource, and which conform to the
requirements of recognised forestry accreditation schemes.

For my mother, the real Julia, whom I miss more than words can say. Her wisdom will always guide me and the memory of her laughter still lifts my spirit and fills my heart with joy.

Also, for Maria, my one and only god-daughter, for Phillipos, who will always be my third boy, and Max, who was my youngest critic and the first to request this sequel.

CHAPTER ONE

Falling for Art

Mediterranean blue! That's the only way I can think to describe the colour of the eyes looking at me from across the room. I have never seen eyes that shade before. My ex-boyfriend, Tom, had piercing blue eyes, and some of the girls at school have them too, but these eyes are different. These eyes are like the sea when the sun is at a certain angle and the colour is so deep that it makes you dizzy to look at it. Oh my God! I can't look away. I'm dizzy and drowning at the same time, looking into this boy's eyes that are . . . come to think of it, looking at me quite persistently from the other side of the room.

Eventually I tear my gaze away from his eyes and look at the rest of him. Dark hair – almost black! How can that be? Black hair and blue eyes? Never heard of that. Dark hair and dark brown eyes, yes. Blond hair and blue eyes, yes – but this is definitely a combination I've never seen before. Black T-shirt, jeans and a dazzling smile directed at me! I look behind me in case there is someone else

1

standing there, in case the smile is meant for them. But no, it appears that he really is looking and smiling at me! I blush and look away, then I look back at him and try to smile too. Suddenly Miss Hughes's voice, which had faded into oblivion while I was swimming in those pools of blue, jolts me back to reality.

'Would you all like to settle down now, please? We will start with a still life in charcoal,' she says, pointing at a rabbit's skull and a piece of driftwood on a slab of marble.

'Mmm, very still,' I think with a giggle, and look over at the boy again, searching for his dreamy blue gaze, to make today's class a little more interesting.

I wish my friend Linda liked art. This class would be so much more fun if she was here too. We always have such a laugh together. But unfortunately art is not really Linda's thing. I did try convincing her to come with me but she wouldn't have any of it. 'It's all right for you, Miss Artistic,' she said to me, after I nagged her for days, 'but I can't even draw a straight line. Besides, it's on a Saturday morning! I can think of better things to do.'

Linda wasn't the only one I had a hard time convincing about the merits of this class. My dad was very resistant to it too. I tried to explain to him that it was my art teacher at school, Miss Mayiou, who had suggested I take this art course. She thinks I'm quite talented, but Dad just said, 'I can understand the benefits of having extra English lessons, but if you are good at art, surely your lessons at school should be sufficient.'

'My teacher says that I can experiment and learn more,' I persisted, 'and besides, it would be good for my English, because I would be speaking with the other kids . . .' I added, knowing that this reasoning might just do the trick.

'That's a good point, Yianni,' my mum said. 'You know how she always speaks Greek when she's around us. It would do her good to have a few more hours of English conversation.' Then she gave me a little wink behind his back. My mum is very keen for me to study art, as she is a frustrated artist herself. She never had the opportunity to study it, so she is determined I will do it for the both of us.

'Well . . .' my dad finally said, not sounding totally convinced, 'so long as you continue with your extra English after school with Miss Hammond on Thursdays. Don't forget you'll be doing English for GCSE as well next year and you still have a long way to go . . .'

Actually, I had thought my English was coming along fine, but I guess he is probably right. I do have a long way to go if I'm going to take any exams here in England. Talking with Linda and the other girls at school is doing wonders for my conversational English, even though I still make them laugh sometimes with my mistakes. But that's not going to be enough if I want good results in my GCSEs.

'Can I sit here?' I hear someone asking, bringing me out of my thoughts. When I turn around to see whose voice it is,

I come face to face with the dreamy blue gaze. He's holding his drawing board under one arm, his paper and charcoal under the other, and at the same time trying to drag a chair towards the table so he can sit next to me.

'Sure,' I mumble, and move over to make space for him.

'My name is Sam,' he says, smiling. 'Who are you?'

Who *am* I? Wow, that's a big question, I think to myself, and then realise he's just asking my name, and not an account of my family lineage or my purpose in life. 'Julia,' I say, blushing and trying to get a grip. Why do I always turn into an idiot when a boy I like talks to me for the first time?

'Have you been here since the beginning?' he asks, as he arranges his materials on the table.

'Yes,' I reply shyly.

'Cool. I've been doing the sculpture class up until now, but I decided to change. Do you go to school near here?'

'No, but I live quite near, so it's easy to come on a Saturday,' I tell him. 'You? Your school is near here?'

'Not far . . . I like your drawings . . .' he says, looking over my shoulder at a page in my sketchbook, which is full of girls' faces, lips, eyes, high-heeled shoes and a million attempts at drawing pretty hands.

'Thanks . . .' I say, blushing again, and trying to discreetly cover the drawings with my hand. 'They're just doodles . . .'

Suddenly I realise that I've been having an actual conversation with someone who hasn't asked me where I come from or what nationality I am. Strange, I think. That's the first thing people usually ask me when they hear my accent. I'm sure he doesn't think I'm British – my English isn't good enough . . . and then my thoughts are interrupted again.

'Now, I want to see from this drawing how you deal with variations in tone,' Mrs Hughes says, then adds rather curtly, 'so concentrate and no talking, please.'

Sam gives me a smile and does something funny with his eyes that makes me want to giggle. Maybe I've found someone to have a laugh with like I do with Linda – only with dreamy blue eyes and a sexy smile. I have a feeling I'm going to enjoy my Saturday mornings even more now.

CHAPTER TWO

What a Difference a Year Makes

The early morning December sun is breaking its way through a misty haze as I make my way on foot to school. I decide not to take the bus from the Tube station today as it's only a few stops, and the sunshine feels like a warm caress on my face. Although it is chilly, the brilliant light lifts my spirits and fills me with a feeling of joy.

'Julia!' I hear some girls from my school calling to me from across the street, and I run to catch up and continue the rest of the journey with them. I walk alongside them, joining in with their cheerful chatter, and once again I'm reminded how different everything was a year ago. It's hard for me to believe that a whole year has gone by already since I first made this school journey. At that time, I did it completely on my own, feeling lonely and isolated; I knew no one. I had arrived from Cyprus only a couple of months before, I spoke no English, and I felt like a complete freak. I used to look with longing at this happy gang of girls walking to school together. I didn't know any of them and couldn't speak their language, so how could I ever imagine joining in? But now I really *do* feel a part of their group.

'How was your weekend?' asks Jane, a friend from my year.

'Brilliant!' I reply, beaming at the memory of Sam with the beautiful eyes.

'What did you do?' she asks, curious about my obvious enthusiasm.

'I had a really good art class on Saturday,' I tell her, quickly realising that this probably doesn't sound that exciting to her.

'And . . . ?' she says, waiting for more.

'And . . . it was great! I like drawing – and there was a really nice boy there too.'

'Ah, so that's what this is about. I thought you already had a boyfriend,' she says, raising her eyebrows at me. 'Aren't you going out with that boy Nima from Tetherlow?'

Having a boyfriend counts for a lot, as far as most of the girls in my school are concerned. So, going out with Nima, who goes to a boys' school near ours, sort of gave me an elevated status – not to mention the fact that quite a few girls knew him and liked him and thought he was really cool.

'I do . . . and I am. I didn't say I was going to go out with this boy – he's just nice . . . makes me laugh,' I reply, hoping that doesn't make me sound fickle. Jane has had the same boyfriend for two years, since she was thirteen, and she says they're going to get engaged next year. As far as Jane is concerned, if you have a boyfriend, you just don't look at other boys. Personally, I think that's stupid when you're only fifteen. 'Anyway,' I carry on, 'just because I have a boyfriend it doesn't mean I can't think another boy is nice too.'

'Well, I suppose so . . .' she says, mulling it over. 'It's just not what I do . . . anyway, what's this boy like?'

'He's got lovely eyes – and he is a great artist,' I tell her, and suddenly I feel a great urge to talk this through with Linda. She'll understand. Since I moved here, Linda's been the only English girl to really understand me. She even understood me when I only spoke about three words of English.

'Oh my God! You did it, didn't you?' Linda says with a gasp, taking a step back and staring hard into my eyes. Her voice drops to a whisper. 'You had sex with Nima!'

Linda's been interrogating me all though lunchtime, trying to find out exactly what happened at the weekend, but I've been having fun not telling her everything, because I love the way Linda gets all flustered when she knows something's up, but can't work out what.

'That's what it is!' she says triumphantly. 'I *knew* it. And that's why you've had that silly smile on your face all day!'

'Linda, honestly! I can't believe you! Is that all you think about?'

'It's not just me! That's all *you* think about too . . . I don't know, Julia. You're acting as if something major happened, so I thought . . . Well, it *could* have been . . . So, WHAT? What happened then?'

'Well . . . I went to my Saturday art class.'

'Big deal. Yeah right, I'm sure that's all that's happened!' she says with a smirk. 'You and your bloody art class!'

'That's not all,' I say, and take a deep breath. 'There was this new boy called Sam and I got talking to him – my stomach was doing that somersault kind of thing I haven't felt since I first met Nima on the bus – or with Tom at Stella's party – and honestly, Linda, for the first time in months I didn't even think of Nima at all on Saturday, and ever since then I keep thinking about Sam and I get this really nice feeling when I do,' I tell her, without pausing for breath.

'Oh no, not again! You are impossible,' Linda says, shaking her head at me. I guess she must be referring to the scrape I got into last year when I met Nima but was still sort of going out with Tom and had to choose between the two.

'What about Nima?' she asks, giving me a dark look.

'Don't worry, I still really like Nima,' I say, and really mean it. 'Nima is the nicest boy I've ever met. If anything he's almost *too* nice . . . Sam's different, though . . . I've just got a bit of a crush on him, that's all. I think it's because he's so artistic. I'll get over it. I'm sure we'll just be good friends. He's really funny – almost as funny as you, actually,' I add, with a big grin. 'Or, come to think of it, maybe even funnier, so you'd better watch out!'

I put my arm through hers and we walk out of the dining hall, giggling.

CHAPTER THREE

Christmas Hysteria

'Eighteen shopping days left till Christmas!' A man's mocking voice shouts from the radio, while I sit at the kitchen table chopping up salad and helping my mother with dinner. 'Better get going, folks – are *you* ready? Have you finished your shopping? Have you wrapped the presents? Have you got the tree? Have you ordered your turkey?'

A pre-Christmas hysteria seems to have gripped London lately, and everywhere you go you are bombarded by it. I find this all a bit excessive. I mean, how many days does a person really need to buy some presents, wrap them and plan a meal? But my usually easygoing mum looks up at me with panic in her eyes when she hears the words 'shopping' and 'turkey'. They are among the few words she understands in English.

'Do you think I should be getting the turkey now too, Ioulia *mou*?' she asks anxiously in Greek. (Ioulia *mou* is what my family call me – it's like saying 'my Julia', only in

11

Greek.) I tell my mum I have absolutely no idea, but I add that it does seem a bit over the top to be buying food that we won't be cooking for nearly three more weeks. Somehow she seems reassured by that logic and she carries on happily with what she's doing.

In Cyprus there is no hysteria around Christmas, and as far as food is concerned, it's usually bought fresh from the market a couple of days before Christmas. A lot of people there buy live chickens and turkeys, which they fatten up for the festive season, although we usually didn't. But my mother preferred to go to the butcher and get her turkey already dead, plucked and ready for cooking. This was probably because, one year, when I was about ten, my dad arrived home from work with a live turkey that someone from his office had given to him as a Christmas gift. He brought it home in the boot of his car, which I thought must have been a wretched journey for a live creature.

'Where did you get that mangy animal?' my mum snapped at my dad when he walked into the house, carrying the terrified bird in both arms. 'And what do you suppose we are going to do with it?'

'Savvas brought it for us from his farm in the village,' he replied, in a cheerful but slightly apologetic voice. 'Imagine how wonderful it will taste. It's been running around the farm all its life, eating only corn and worms . . . We'll keep it for a couple of weeks and fatten it up for Christmas.'

'Where do you propose we keep it and who is going to

feed it to fatten it up?' Mum continued, still in a very loud voice, because she knew she would be the one to carry the burden as usual. 'We don't live in the village and we don't have a farm for it to run around in – or haven't you noticed?'

'We'll keep it in the garage, and I'll make a chicken coop for it,' he replied.

'And could you please tell me who is going to clean up all its mess and then kill it when the time comes?' By now my mum's voice was getting even louder and I was sure that the whole street could hear her.

'I'll do it,' Dad replied reluctantly, knowing full well that it was the only thing he could possibly say.

We did keep the turkey for a couple of weeks in the garage, and my father, true to his word, fattened it up nicely by feeding it all the best bits from our leftovers, cleaned its mess, visited it regularly to check it was OK . . . and, as a result, became rather fond of the poor animal.

The night before Christmas Eve, when the time came to kill it, my dad walked into the garage armed with a big knife to do the 'deed', while we waited for him in the kitchen, my mum equipped with the necessary tools to start de-feathering the poor bird as soon as he finished. Twenty minutes later, he reappeared, still holding the knife, but there were no signs of slaughter on it.

He collapsed on a chair at the kitchen table and held

his head in his hands. Then he looked up at the three of us and said, in a barely audible voice, 'I can't do it . . . How can I cut his throat? He was so pleased to see me! He looked at me with his little eyes, thinking I had come to feed him. How can I possibly kill him?'

But my mother wouldn't have any of it, and half an hour later, after a couple of stiff whiskies, my dad ventured back into the garage. He returned nearly an hour later, with a still unsoiled knife and moist eyes.

'I'm not a murderer!' he shouted, slammed the knife on the table and slumped in the kitchen chair again.

A Christmas lunch of only salad and potatoes and a big fat turkey as a permanent pet looked like a very real possibility that year . . . That is, until my mum made a phone call to my grandfather, who dutifully came round the next morning to kill the turkey for us. Everyone enjoyed that year's organic turkey – apart from my dad. He stuck to the potatoes and salad . . .

Giggling at the memory, I remind my mother of our favourite Christmas story and we have a good laugh at my father's expense. By now, he's learned to live with the teasing.

As Christmas carols and advertising jingles cheerfully blare out of the radio, I realise that I don't actually remember any of this from last year. I vaguely remember some Christmas trees and fairy lights in the streets, but this whole manic, hysterical thing just passed me by. I guess for me, last year's festive season was altogether a bit of a let-down, even though we shared a house with my friend Anna and her family. We were all still very homesick for Cyprus.

This year, however, we have all made up our minds to have a brilliant time. We'll have a tree, lights, presents, parties, lots of food . . . We are going to celebrate Christmas just like the English do! This, I have discovered, mainly involves having a lot more Christmas decorations around the house.

Sam's English, I think to myself and a sudden flash of his sexy smile comes to mind just out of the blue. I wonder what sort of Christmas he'll be having with his English family and if they'll have a ton of decorations around their house. I find, to my surprise, that ever since I met Sam, he keeps creeping into my thoughts when I least expect it.

'Are you going to buy Nima a Christmas present, Ioulia *mou*?' my mum asks, bringing me out of my Sam daydream.

'I hadn't really thought about it yet, Mama, but yes, I will,' I say, and I start wondering what to get him . . .

'And something nice for Anna so we can all exchange gifts at our Christmas party,' my mum reminds me.

My mum loves parties and she is brilliant at throwing them, so we decided we'd have a big Christmas lunch at our new flat and invite all the people we've met and liked since we've been in England. Since we only arrived here a year and half ago, we're not exactly going to have hundreds of guests, but I know my mum – one way or another, between her and Anna's mum, *Kyria* Eva, they'll gather enough people together to have a really good time.

Last year we shared a house with another family from Cyprus. Mrs Seferis (*Kyria* Eva), Mr Seferis (*Kyrios* Petros) and their son and daughter Stavros and Anna. When we moved to Hampstead, Mum and *Kyria* Eva kept up a really close friendship, just like Anna and I have, despite the fact that Anna is two years older than I am. We understand each other and share so much, because we come from the same place, have had the same experiences and speak the same native language. Anna loves living in London as much as I do now, but Cyprus is in our blood and we miss it and still long to go back there. She is the only one of my friends who can truly understand this because she feels exactly the same. I can tell Linda about my country and about my family and friends in Cyprus, but it's hard for her to really know what I'm talking about. I've decided I want to take Linda to Cyprus some day, so she can see for herself how beautiful it is.

I still miss so many things about my life there – especially my cousin Sophia, my other relatives and my cat, Chloe. I can't believe I haven't been back for a whole year and a half. I wonder if Chloe will still know who I am? Sometimes everything seems like a dream and I don't know where the dream stops and reality starts. Does Cyprus really exist, or is it just a place in my dreams? Or perhaps I just dreamed that we left Cyprus for London. And sometimes when I wake up, I expect to be in my bed in our house in Nicosia. When I dream at night, it's often about my *bapu*, my gandfather. Although I long to visit everyone I left behind, my grandfather is old and I worry that I might not see him again if I don't go back soon. My grandfather was the most disappointed out of everyone when I decided not to go home for Christmas this year. But I told him summer will come quickly and I'll be there for the whole of the holidays and spend lots of time with him then.

There are also special places in Cyprus that I dream about, and sometimes I wake up crying. I know it's silly, but I can't help it, it just happens. There is one particular place that my cousin Sophia and I used to go to when we were little, and I dream about it all the time. It was a little plot of land next to our house that hadn't been built on yet, where the two of us used to go and play. We built a little house of our own there, with branches, stones and some old sheets my mum gave us, and we'd take our dolls and some bread and olives and pretend that it was where we lived. In the winter and spring, the ground would be covered in lovely moist green grass and wildflowers, so we'd pick lots of flowers for our little house. Yellow, blue and mauve anemones were our favourite. We'd play there for hours and sit in the winter sunshine, but we never went there in the summer. It was far too hot and we were frightened of the snakes. I wonder if it still exists? I'll ask Sophia next time I write and maybe we can go back there this summer. Mum told me that even if she and Dad and my brother Tony don't go, I can spend the summer with Sophia. I can't wait!

'What's for dinner?' Tony calls out, bringing me out of my thoughts – it's his coming-home mantra – as the door slams behind him.

'Fried aubergines and salad,' my mum calls back. 'Hope you're hungry!'

'Starving!' replies Tony, and I laugh, since I've never known him to be anything but starving. He ruffles my hair as he passes me, and as I watch my brother make his way to the stove, still wearing his winter coat and gloves, smelling of the cold London air, I know this is not a dream. This is my life now, here in this country, in this cosy little flat in London with my family.

CHAPTER FOUR

Boys and Girls

Since the boys' school is so close to ours, Linda and I usually meet up with Nima and his friend Ali after school to catch the bus together. The four of us are excitedly discussing the New Year's Eve party Nima has planned for this year, but two old ladies on the bus are giving us dirty looks and tutting with obvious irritation. 'Young people today,' I hear one say to the other, with a rather loud sigh. 'No consideration or respect for others.'

I don't think that's true, and their attitude really bothers me because we are not being rude, disrespectful or hurting anyone. We're just happy and cheerful, even if we are a bit noisy. Why can't they see that? In Cyprus, it always seemed that older people and younger people enjoy each other's company. I feel sorry for these two old women, who, I think, seem unhappy and I try to ignore them.

Nima has overcome the first hurdle of convincing his parents to let him have a New Year's party, so now we are just working out the details. The party is going to be a great adventure and the first proper party I'll be involved in organising since coming to London. I know that Linda is hoping it might be an opportunity for her to get off with Ali, as she really fancies him. She keeps waiting for him to ask her out. I suggested to her that perhaps she ought to let him know that she likes him in that way, but Linda is shy around boys. 'We're such good friends,' she said the other day, 'so it's really awkward. I don't know how to let him know I'd like us to be more than *just* friends.' We've been making a list of who we'd like to invite and part of me wants to invite Sam too, although I haven't mentioned it to anyone yet. He's such a lot of fun it'd be great to have him there, but the more I think about it, the more it doesn't seem like a good idea. I try to visualise Sam and Nima being at the same party and I start to feel nauseous and extremely nervous, so I soon dismiss that particular idea.

'Do you want to go Christmas shopping?' Nima asks me a little later, when Linda and Ali have got off the bus.

'OK. When do you want to go?'

'How about Saturday? There's not much time left before Christmas and I haven't bought anything yet.'

Oh no! Nima's been listening to that hysterical man on the radio, I think, and smile to myself.

'What are you grinning at?' he asks smiling back at me.

'Oh, nothing – it's just everyone seems to have gone

hysterical about Christmas shopping,' I tell him and reach over to brush aside a bit of hair that's fallen over his eyes. I love Nima's shiny black hair, which he pulls back in a ponytail, and his beautiful brown eyes with thick, long eyelashes that most girls would kill for. I think he looks really exotic. Suddenly, without warning, I get a flash of Sam's mesmerising blue eyes and his wicked smile and I think how different they are. It also occurs to me how strange it is to be attracted to two boys who are so different from each other – and not just in the way they look. Most girls I know talk about types of boy they fancy. If these two are anything to go by, I don't think I have a type.

'So how about going shopping on Saturday?' Nima says.

'Well . . .' I say, hesitating and feeling a little flustered, because I can't get the image of Sam out of my head. 'I go to my art classes on Saturday, remember?'

'Oh yeah, I forgot,' he says, playfully slapping his head with his hand and releasing the bit of hair I just brushed back over. 'But that's in the morning, isn't it? How about Saturday afternoon?'

'OK, I'll do my homework on Sunday,' I reply. 'I'll meet you by Hampstead Tube around three, and we can go to the West End.'

It's always a surprise when I hear myself say things like that. I can't believe how comfortable I am with going into the centre of London these days, and with my boyfriend! Eight months ago, not only could I not use the Tube on my own, I couldn't even *spell* it! And there was no way my parents would have allowed me to go anywhere with a boy who wasn't my brother. Actually, my parents didn't give me too hard a time about going out with Nima, which was a bit of a shock. They seem to really like him and treat him very politely – though my brother just ignores him. But even though she trusts and likes Nima, my mum still tries to encourage me not to get too serious. 'You are too young for a serious relationship, Ioulia *mou*,' she reminds me at regular intervals.

Before Nima, my parents had always made it clear that if I had a boyfriend, they'd like him to be Greek, but somehow they're OK with Nima – they've met his parents and I'm certain the main reason is that even though they are Iranian, Nima's dad used to work in Athens and speaks some Greek. I think this has lulled them into the illusion he actually is Greek. It also helps that our two sets of parents seem to like each other, which isn't really surprising, I suppose, as they have the same values and similar ideas about life and all that, but even so, I know my mum. She would still prefer it if he actually *was* Greek.

Although this has made things relatively easy with Nima, it does annoy me a little, because I know for sure that if I was going out with an English boy it would be a very different story. For example, if Sam asked me out and I decided to go, I'd have to do it behind their backs; it would cause too much trouble and tension if I tried to explain. I can just hear it now: 'What do you want with an English boy? They are so different from us, they expect different things from girls and you are not old enough for that kind of thing . . .' blah, blah, blah . . . Not to mention what my brother would go on about! He doesn't think I'm old enough to go out with anybody who is not a girl. Anyway, I'm sure Sam's not going to ask me out . . . and besides, I'm going out with Nima who is lovely and I definitely wouldn't want to hurt him.

CHAPTER FIVE

Sleep! Glorious Sleep!

When you're a young Greek person, you sleep late in the mornings and no one minds. When you are older, you have siestas and no one minds. I have discovered that most of my English friends are not allowed to stay in bed late, even when they don't have school, because apparently it's a sign of laziness and it's not good for you. But I don't have to worry about my parents thinking I'm lazy or unhealthy staying in bed as long as I do. On the contrary, they believe sleep is an essential part of a person's well-being and should be encouraged. My parents tiptoe around when my brother Tony and I are asleep, and if the phone rings, it's picked up quickly so as not to disturb us.

My friends in London used to ring me early at the weekends, and my mother was always having to explain to them that I was in bed – until they finally got the message. 'Julia, she sleeps,' was one of the first English sentences she learned to say.

'You are so lucky,' Linda told me early in our friendship. 'My mum thinks I'm "idle" and a "slob", if I stay in bed all morning.'

'It's cultural,' I replied, feeling proud of myself for using such an intelligent word.

Considering how much I cherish these Saturday lie-ins, it's quite amazing that I haven't minded getting up for my art classes. I guess it's an indication of how much I love going to the class, though the prospect of seeing Sam might have a little to do with it too. Still, I do have all Sunday morning to make up for lost sleep.

School days, like today, are another story. It's my dad who has the thankless task of waking me up. Since he's always up first, I don't need an alarm clock. It always feels like he's dragging me out of a delicious deep sleep, usually in the middle of a dream. Although, of course, I love my dad, at that moment when he calls my name in the morning, I just hate him. He's always so gentle and sweet, and when I don't respond to his call, he comes into my room and softly brushes the hair off my face with his warm hand and quietly says my name. But I *still* hate him for waking me. I want him to disappear and leave me alone, so I always grunt and dive under the bedclothes.

Of course I do eventually get up and love him again. Since I usually feel groggy when I first wake up and can never eat anything that early in the morning, there is always a mug of steaming hot chocolate waiting for me on the kitchen table when I finally appear. I sip it as my dad sits at the table and shaves, a ritual I have been watching ever since I started school at the age of five. A little transistor radio sits with him, broadcasting the news, and next to it sits a bowl of hot water with a funny little bristly brush in it. He uses the brush to make lots of white foam on a bar of shaving soap, then to cover his face with the foam. It always makes me laugh because he looks like Father Christmas with his white beard. Then, looking into a small mirror that stands on the table, he very carefully and slowly shaves it all off with an old-fashioned razor. My mum and my brother have been trying for years to get him to use an electric razor but he won't do it. I'm glad because it's comforting to watch and gives me time to wake up gently before going off to school.

The Christmas spirit seems to have an intoxicating effect on all of us at school and no one can concentrate on anything much. As far as the girls are concerned, the Christmas holidays are practically here and luckily for us, most of the teachers seem to have entered into the spirit of things too.

All the Years have been preparing acts to perform in front of the rest of the school in our annual Christmas show, and our Year has been putting together a few humorous sketches, which we've had to devise ourselves. We have been working on different ideas for weeks now.

In Cyprus I always took part in the plays and shows at school because, apart from art, drama was my favourite subject. But since I've been in England, this is the first opportunity I've had to participate. Not being able to speak English when I came here seriously hindered my acting ability! But this year Linda and Scarlet, the nice new girl who joined our class halfway through term, encouraged me to act in the show, especially after I came up with a possible idea for one of the sketches. Unlike last year, when I got myself into a huge muddle by inadvertently agreeing to run for the school on sports day, this time I am well aware of what I'm letting myself in for.

Over the weekend, I thought of a new idea, which I struggle to describe to everyone during our drama lesson. It's something I once saw on a comedy programme on Cypriot television about a woman who is undressing behind a screen. We don't get to see the woman, just her hand, which appears for short intervals over the screen in order to hang items of clothing over the edge. She's doing this to the sound of loud music, like in a strip show. The clothes keep coming off, one item at a time until finally her stockings, suspenders, sexy knickers and bra are all hanging over the edge. Then, the camera moves round behind the screen to reveal the woman, who turns out to be a totally *un*sexy middle-aged housewife. She's standing, not naked as expected, but wearing her apron and slippers sorting out a pile of laundry, with an old transistor radio perched on top of a washing machine, blaring out the music.

The girls and our teacher think the idea is hilarious, so we decide to go ahead with it. As it's a non-speaking part and everyone seems to want me to do the part of the woman I nervously accept. Although my English seems to be just fine these days when I talk with my friends, the idea of standing up and saying anything in front of the whole school makes me break out into a sweat. I accept only because I don't have a single word to say and hope it will go down well with all the other kids.

'I'm going to be in the school play, for Christmas,' I tell my mum that evening while laying the table for dinner.

'That's nice, Ioulia *mou*,' she says, smiling at me. 'Are you doing a nativity play? Do you have to learn lots of words?'

'No, Mama,' I tell her, giggling, then I remind her of the mock striptease scene we watched together on TV, and explain that I'll be doing it on stage.

'Did your teacher think that was a suitable thing for a Christmas show?' she asks in amazement.

'Everyone thought it was very funny and liked it a lot,' I tell her.

'Your daughter is scandalising her school,' she tells my dad later on at dinner with a big grin on her face and proceeds to explain to him and my brother about the Christmas show. My mum thinks I'm a bit of a free spirit, which she likes, providing I keep it under control. I wonder what she'd say if she knew that I'm always fantasising about an English boy called Sam, even though I have a boyfriend called Nima . . .

'Typical!' Tony says, stuffing a huge piece of feta cheese in his mouth. 'I wondered how long it was going to take her before she started misbehaving. Not speaking English suited you a lot better, little Miss Mischief.'

While they are all talking and eating, I'm drifting off on one of my daydreams about Sam, then I feel guilty about being attracted to him when I have Nima, which puts me right off my dinner. Now not only do I have to watch what I tell my family, but I have to hide my thoughts from Nima too. And that's dishonest, isn't it? It's always been so easy to talk to Nima, but ever since Sam made an appearance in my life I have felt so unsettled. How can I feel this way after only just meeting Sam? Being with him gave me such a buzz – he seems so mysterious and exciting. Being with Nima has always been safe and comfortable, which is one of the things I really like about him. But what does it mean for us if I'm having feelings like this for someone else?

'What's the matter, Ioulia *mou*? Are you all right?' my mum asks, noticing that, unlike my brother, I've stopped stuffing my face. 'Why have you stopped eating?'

Of course, to stop eating is the worst thing you can do if you don't want to attract any attention in this household. The second you do that, my mother starts asking questions and taking your temperature. 'Are you feeling all right?' she asks me again.

'I'm fine, Mama, please. I'm just tired,' I say and force another mouthful of pasta down my throat just to keep her off my back. When I'm in this frame of mind what I need most is to go and see Anna for a chat and get her mum to read my coffee grounds. My mum is quite good at it too, but *Kyria* Eva is the best! She just seems to get it spot on, and she always has some good advice for my problems and dilemmas somehow – as if she knows what's going on in my life. I mean, how could she know? It's so spooky! I have no idea how this reading coffee grounds thing actually works. We just sit around chatting about absolutely nothing and drinking coffee and then when we finish, we turn our cups upside down on their saucers and wait for the grounds to dry. When they're ready she puts her glasses on, turns the cup over and starts looking into the cup and sees all these incredible things that just seem to totally relate to what is happening in my life, or Anna's. I'm convinced it's magic. Maybe *Kyria* Eva is a witch – a really nice witch, of course – or, at the very least, she is truly blessed with the gift of fortune-telling.

We have a lot of people like that in our culture, always have. There was a woman in ancient Greece called Pythia and she was known as The Sacred Oracle. People would go on pilgrimages from all across the land to hear her predictions. She used to sit on a stool over a boiling vat of something or other, chewing some kind of leaf that made her go into a trance – I think she was probably stoned or drunk or something – and then started talking in riddles. I guess *Kyria* Eva is like a modern-day Pythia. Of course, she isn't stoned or drunk and she doesn't go into a trance, but her eyes do glaze over a bit when she is looking into the cup . . .

CHAPTER SIX

Language Lesson

'Hi Julia!' Sam's voice greets me as I walk into art class on Saturday morning. He's leaning nonchalantly against a table, where the teacher has carefully set up another still life for us to draw. This time the still life is a selection of fruit and vegetables in a big wicker basket, like the sort my auntie Eleni would use for her shopping on market days in Cyprus.

'How's it going?' he asks me in his deep, sexy voice as I walk towards him, but before I get a chance to reply, the teacher's shrill voice makes us all jump.

'Would you be kind enough not to lean on the table, please?' she says, glaring at Sam and pointing at him with her finger in front of everyone. I'm really embarrassed for him, but then I see him pull a face and make a rude gesture behind her back and he heads for his seat. Feeling better for him, I suppress a smile and go over to sit down next to him.

While I get my things ready on the table in order to

start my drawing, I consider what the teacher has just said to Sam and I find her choice of words very strange. The words she used were so contradictory to her message. 'Would you be kind enough . . .' To me, that seems like a very polite way of asking someone *to* do something, but it was obvious from the tone of her voice that she was not being at all friendly or polite. She was angry. I decide it's just another one of those peculiarities in the English language that I have to get used to if I don't want to get the wrong message.

My family had quite a laugh when Yiorgos, one of my grown-up cousins, got himself into a similar language muddle. He came to London to surprise his student girlfriend who was living with an English family. When he turned up at her flat, the mother of the family said, in what seemed to him like a very concerned tone, 'I'm terribly sorry, I am afraid Thalia is not here.' Yiorgos thought something terrible had happened to Thalia. Phrases like 'I'm afraid', and 'terribly sorry', delivered in a grave voice can send the wrong message to someone who's not very familiar with the language! Yiorgos thought his beloved had either died or was seriously ill in hospital. It didn't occur to him that she might just be out shopping. Why would the woman be so 'terribly sorry' and so very 'afraid'? He eventually found out what it all meant, but not till he came to our house in a terrible state and my brother explained.

'God, she's a real pain,' Sam whispers to me when the

teacher is in another part of the room helping somebody with their drawing. 'She's so bloody stressed out! I know what *she* needs, but I'm not volunteering . . .'

After class, Sam and I walk together to the bus stop.

'What are you doing for Christmas?' Sam asks me as we wait for the bus. The art class has broken up now, so we won't be going back until the new year. The deep tone of Sam's voice makes him sound more like a man than a boy. When he talks to me, it sort of makes me go weak and pathetic and sends a thrill down to the pit of my stomach.

'Spending it with my family,' I tell him, trying to sound as grown up as I can whilst making sure I don't squeak nervously. 'What about you?'

'Same,' he says, taking a cigarette out of his packet of Camel Lights and lighting it. I stare at him as he flicks his Zippo lighter closed and puts it back in his jeans pocket. That probably explains the gravelly voice despite the fact that he's only seventeen, I think, staring at him. None of my friends smokes – apart from my cousin Sophia, and she only pretends. She tried to show me how to do it once last summer, but it made me gag, so I never tried it again.

'Oh, sorry, Julia,' he says, when he sees me staring at him. 'Would you like one?'

'No, thanks, I don't smoke,' I reply.

'Anyway, New Year's Eve is a much more significant

celebration as far as I'm concerned,' he carries on. 'I much prefer it. What are you doing this year?'

'Going to a party,' I say a bit reluctantly. I suddenly realise I don't want to talk about Nima, so I desperately try to think of something else to say to change the subject. Unfortunately nothing comes to mind.

'Do you want to meet up during the holidays?' he asks, as he exhales his cigarette smoke, apparently oblivious to the fact that I'm totally tongue-tied. 'Give me your number and I'll call you sometime.'

'S-sure,' I manage to say while my stomach is doing some spectacular acrobatics and my heart is pounding so hard I think he can see my coat pulsating. God! Is Sam asking me out or is he trying to be friends? I don't know which it is. This is all so new to me. I know I fancy him but that doesn't mean he fancies me . . . he probably just likes me and wants to be friends which is fine by me, and either way I'm ecstatic and flying high with happiness. In fact, I'm so happy that suddenly I'm struck down by total amnesia and I forget everything and everyone else in my life – like Nima, for example.

'What are you doing this afternoon?' he says. 'There's a great exhibition of surrealist art at the Tate I'm thinking of going to. Do you want to come?'

'Oh no, I can't today . . .' I reply with a sinking heart, and clipped wings. I'm lost for words about what to say next because I don't want to tell him that I have a date with my boyfriend this afternoon. I'm also acutely aware that, yet again, I'm not mentioning Nima. I just don't want to tell Sam that I have a boyfriend, which doesn't exactly make me feel great about myself. It feels dishonest and Nima's lovely face comes to mind and makes me feel doubly bad. I know I'm playing a game, but it would be so brilliant to do something with Sam, and besides, I've been so desperate to go to an exhibition in London, even if I'm not sure what surrealist art is exactly. I guess what I'm afraid of is that he might be put off asking me to go with him if he knew I had a boyfriend. Anyway, I don't know why I'm being so paranoid about mentioning Nima, because a boy like Sam probably has a girlfriend – or a dozen, more likely.

'I've got to get home and then I'm going Christmas shopping,' I finally hear myself say.

'Christmas shopping, eh?' he says as we line up to get on the bus. 'What a pain that is! I can't believe all the materialism and commercialism that goes on at this time of year. Christmas is supposed to be a religious celebration.' He flicks his cigarette on to the pavement and stubs it out with the heel of his trainer. 'Not that I care much about religion or anything, but the whole thing has become a circus as far as I'm concerned. But no problem . . . that's cool. We can do it another time.'

'That'd be good,' I say, relieved at the suggestion of another time, and making a mental note to look up 'surrealist art' as soon as I get home.

* * *

I'm overheating and out of breath when I reach the top of the hill to meet Nima outside Hampstead Tube. I glance at my watch and realise I'm half an hour late, and it's already starting to get dark.

'I was worried you weren't coming,' he tells me, as we make our way into the Underground.

'Sorry, Nima,' I say, still breathless from running. 'I got involved with helping my mum put up some Christmas lights after lunch, and I thought I was never going to get out of the house.'

'No worries,' he says, and takes my hand. 'We've got loads of time. The shops stay open till late.'

I look at Nima and feel a rush of affection. I don't need to worry about anything when I'm with him. Unlike being around Sam, when I'm with Nima my heart is not pounding, my stomach is not somersaulting and I'm not wracked with guilt about everything.

The sight of Oxford Street and Regent Street nearly makes me gasp as we emerge from the Underground at Oxford Circus. Although I've now done this trip millions of times since I've been in England, the sight of central London still thrills me. But I have never seen it looking more beautiful than this. In fact, I have never seen anything so beautiful and festive as this in my whole life. Last Christmas I kept well away from the centre of London – it seemed far too scary to me then. In the summer I enjoyed walking the streets, especially in the bright sunshine, with my friends. But it just didn't compare with this Christmas fairyland of lights, tinsel and colour.

'Wow, Nima!' I say, squeezing his hand and gazing at everything sparkling around me. 'This is truly amazing. Just like in the movies.'

'I keep forgetting this is all new to you,' he says sweetly. 'We all take it for granted because we live here and see it every year.'

All the shops are so brightly lit, overflowing with stuff – decorations, toys, jewellery, clothes, make-up . . . Everything imaginable seems to be wrapped up and transformed into a Christmas gift in the shop windows. I feel like I have never seen so much *stuff* in all my life . . . Each shop seems more lavishly decorated than the last, all of them competing with each other to attract customers. Eventually, as my eyes get used to the plethora of colours and lights, my initial excitement subsides and I become aware of the spending frenzy that has gripped the city and it all starts to make me feel dizzy. Sam's words from this morning echo in my ears. He's right, I think, Christmas shouldn't be just about material things. Everyone seems to have gone mad.

CHAPTER SEVEN

An Irresistible Proposition

The ringing of the telephone makes me jump out of my skin and snaps me out of my homework blues. I hear my brother answer it in the other room before I get the chance to pick it up. It's Sunday and I'm looking for any excuse to stop doing this boring homework that has got me up early and has kept me cooped up in my bedroom all morning. The only consolation is that it is the last bit of homework we have to give in this term.

'Julia, it's for you!' shouts Tony and I run to the phone, expecting to hear Linda's voice. To my surprise, a male voice greets me instead.

'Hi Julia, it's Sam,' he says cheerfully.

Wow! Sam! I didn't expect to hear from him so soon. My heart starts to pound like mad and the blood rushes to my face, colouring it crimson.

'How're you doing?' he carries on, before I get a chance to say anything. 'Do you want to go to that exhibition I told you about yesterday?'

'Oh, hi,' I say, trying to sound cool, 'I thought you were going yesterday.'

'Yeah, I know, but I didn't get round to it. What're you doing now? Do you want to come today?'

'I'm doing my homework,' I reply, trying to steady my voice, 'But yes, I'd like to come. When are you going?'

'When you finish your homework,' he says with a smile in his voice. 'Do you want me to come round and pick you up?'

'Oh no,' I say and get into a panic just thinking about having to explain to Tony or my parents who he is. 'Don't worry, I'll meet you somewhere, I'm almost finished.'

'Cool,' he says. 'Do you want to meet outside Camden Tube in an hour?'

'OK, see you at twelve,' I reply a bit shakily. As I put the receiver down I realise I don't have his number in case something goes wrong, so I keep my fingers crossed that Tony doesn't give me the third degree about where I'm going and with whom and make me late.

'Who was that?' my brother asks as I walk out of the room, 'Never heard *his* voice before . . .'

'Oh, just a friend,' I tell him, trying to sound indifferent. Honestly, when is my brother going to stop being so protective? Probably not till I'm married with five kids and living in another country. Doesn't he realise that I'm fifteen now, we live in England, and I can take care of myself perfectly well?

I quickly finish my homework and look up 'surrealism'

in my English-to-Greek dictionary. I can't find it in there, so I have to look it up in my English one, which is altogether trickier. *Surrealism – a movement in art and literature involving the combination of incongruous images, as in a dream.* Then I have to look up 'incongruous' since I have no idea what *that* means. There's nothing in there about either word deriving from Greek (so many English words do, which has helped me learn the language) so that probably explains why I'd never heard of them.

As I'm getting ready, I make a call to Linda and ask her to cover for me. Luckily, my parents are out so I can just leave them a note saying I've gone to meet her. I feel better not having to lie straight to their faces. I just wish my parents weren't so strict and unreasonable about my friendships with boys, then I wouldn't have to lie at all. When will they understand that boys are only human too, and that they are not all waiting to pounce on me or do me harm? Then I just have to slip out the door before Tony sees me.

A blast of hot air and the unmistakable smell of the Underground hit us as we run down the escalator at Camden Town Tube station. It's an exhilarating feeling. On the platform the noise from the trains, the gust of wind that blows from the tunnels and the dozens of visual images that surround me all compete for my attention. But Sam is the most interesting of all.

'Look at that poster,' Sam says, pointing at a huge

picture of a cup, saucer and spoon made out of fur. 'That's the exhibition we're going to see,' he says and I stare at it in disbelief. What an incredible image! I have never seen anything like it in my life. What a strange concept! I suppose that's what the dictionary meant by *incongruous*, and I start to understand a bit about the concept of surrealism.

'Meret Oppenheim did that in the 1930s. It's called *Breakfast in Fur*,' Sam explains. 'But my favourite artist is Salvador Dali. He's so wicked.'

None of this makes much sense to me, but I nod. I like what I see on the poster – the image makes me smile. It would be a very messy job trying to drink coffee from it – and my mum and *Kyria* Eva would certainly not be able to read anyone's coffee grounds in it either!

CHAPTER EIGHT

Deep and Troubled Waters

'So, what did you think of that?' Sam asks me, lighting up a cigarette once we're out of the Tate Gallery.

My head is buzzing, and I'm trying to compose my thoughts on the exhibition, let alone Sam. I can honestly say that I have just spent two hours looking at the most incredible things I have ever seen and Sam was fantastic, showing me around and explaining everything. He was very knowledgeable about art and was so sweet and nice, taking the time to point things out to me. I loved being with him and I love surrealist art!

A crowd of young people are sitting on the steps of the gallery chatting, smoking and drinking coffee from the mobile café that's parked at the bottom of the steps. Sam seems to know most of them and they call out for us to join them. The winter sun is breaking through the clouds and even though it's cold, the air from the river feels fresh and crisp, and we sit bathed in warm sunlight.

'This is Julia,' Sam says, introducing me to his friends

all at once. 'She goes to the same art class as me.' Everyone is friendly and nice and they all discuss the exhibition animatedly and seem to know a lot about art too. I feel really ignorant and very aware that I know so little, so I listen and promise myself I will learn all I can because art is what I love best.

'A couple of my friends said they'd be here,' Sam explains to me as they discuss Dali, 'but I didn't realise they'd all come.'

'They seem really nice,' I tell him.

As people start to get up and walk down the steps, Sam leans over to me. 'Everyone's going to Ed's house for coffee. Do you have to get back home, or can you come for a bit?'

'OK, I'll come for a bit,' I say, a little hesitantly. 'Where does he live?'

'Belsize Park,' he replies and pulls me off the steps with both hands, sending a thrill down my spine.

Ed lives in a flat with four other people who are all students.

'Ed's lucky,' Sam tells me as we sit down on some cushions on the floor in the sitting room. 'This flat belongs to his grandmother, and she lets him have it really cheap.' He stubs out yet another cigarette in the already overflowing ashtray. 'It's not exactly a slum, is it? I wouldn't mind having a place like this when I go to art school. Can't wait to leave school and leave home.'

'Who wants coffee, and who wants beer?' asks Scott, one of Ed's flatmates.

'Coffee, please,' I say shyly, as Laura, Ed's girlfriend, comes over and sits next to me on the floor. She's got a ruby-coloured nose stud and shoulder-length dreadlocks, and is wearing dozens of silver bangles that jingle musically when she moves. The light is fading fast outside so Laura gets up and starts lighting scented candles around the room. The two lava lamps which were switched on earlier are already starting to mesmerise me with their glowing performance, throwing shades of blue, purple and red all over the room and on everyone's faces. Suddenly, I hear the gentle sound of someone strumming a guitar. I look around and see a guy sitting cross-legged on the sofa behind me playing an acoustic guitar while the girl next to him is nibbling his ear. The music is lovely and mellow and he soon starts singing.

The last time I was in the same room with someone playing the guitar and singing was last Easter when we had a family party and one of our relatives was playing Greek songs and we were all doing Greek dancing. I think how different this is as the laid-back sound of reggae fills the room.

Laura has finished lighting candles and I try to make out what she's doing now. She's got a tin box with tobacco in it and another one with what looks like the herb oregano, which my mum uses when she makes Greek salad with feta cheese. Laura also has some cigarette

45

papers, which she licks and sticks together to make into one big long paper. She then spreads it out on the coffee table and proceeds to fill it up with tobacco, which she sprinkles with some oregano. Finally she rolls the paper up, making it into what looks like a very rough-looking and rather large cigarette.

Suddenly, like a thunderbolt, I realise what I'm witnessing in person, for the first time in my life. Laura's cigarette is not sprinkled with oregano at all, but marijuana. I stare at Laura as she strikes a match and lights the roll-up, sucking hard on it to make sure it's well lit. Once on its way, Laura takes a few deep drags and the pungent smell and smoke fill the room making me cough. Then Laura passes it on to the guy with the guitar, who, thanking her politely, does the same, passing it on to the girl who stops nibbling his ear for a bit while she smokes and then she passes it on too. I stare in absolute amazement at this ritual and think how unhygienic it is.

Then I become aware that I'm sitting in a circle of people happily smoking marijuana like it's the most natural thing in the world, and I start to feel very anxious and nervous.

I watch the spliff making its way around the group and I start to worry about what I should do or say when it comes to me, and I break into a sweat. The smoke and the panic cloud my thoughts, but, although inside I'm in a real state, I try to keep my cool in front of Sam. I don't want to embarrass myself or make him think I'm an idiot.

What I really want to do is get up and walk out, but I know I can't do that. All I can think of is what my parents would say if they knew where I was, and that my brother would kill me if he found out. Then it strikes me that I'm witnessing something illegal and my extremely active imagination starts to go into overdrive. I begin to visualise a police raid, with sirens, flashing lights, the whole lot, and I see me sitting in the police station explaining myself in front of my family. Oh God! Why did I get myself into this mess? This is even more panic-inducing than the time I was with Tom at Stella's party and we were kissing on the bed with the coats and I was trying to stop him putting his hand up my skirt . . .

Sam has the cigarette now and after he takes a few deep drags from it, he leans over, smiling, and slips a hand around my waist, then offers it to me.

'I know you don't smoke, but don't you want some of *this*?' he says, exhaling smoke into my face. That's it, I think with relief – and try not to cough – that's my excuse! I don't smoke.

'No thanks,' I say with a broad smile, keeping very cool. 'I'd rather not. Do you mind?'

'No problem,' he says, taking another drag, and then he passes it on to the guy on the sofa again. Phew! That was stressful, I think, and wipe my sweaty palms on my jeans.

Walking home in the clear cold night with the bright moon shining above us, the atmosphere between Sam and me is electric. As we walk really close to each other I can feel a warmth radiating from Sam's body like a heater and every time I look at him I can see his blue eyes shining and glistening in the moonlight. Neither of us says much, but somehow we don't need to talk.

Just before turning into my road Sam leans over, wraps an arm around my waist and pulls me towards him. And suddenly, like in a dream, I find myself kissing him. For what seems like hours.

CHAPTER NINE

Danger, Danger

Luckily, when I get home, my parents and Tony are out. I feel really nervous and my heart is pounding so hard it feels like it's trying to jump out of my chest. I ran like mad the rest of the way home because I was worried I'd be late and have to explain myself. Once in the house I quickly change my clothes and barricade myself in my small bedroom with a glass of milk and a halloumi cheese sandwich, not that I can drink or eat anything, but I know when my mum comes home she is going to interrogate me about what I've eaten.

I just can't face talking to my family right now. I need to think about everything that happened today and unravel my feelings, so I take refuge in the safety of my bedroom. Getting into bed seems to be the best place for doing my thinking, probably because it's the only place I can block out the rest of the world. As it's too early for sleep, I open my books with the pretence of doing homework but start drawing instead. I always draw when

I'm trying to think things through. It relaxes me and lets my mind wander off in a way that helps me make sense of how I feel, and right now confused is the most appropriate way to describe how I feel.

What an incredible day it's been! My mind keeps going over all the events, like a scene from a movie, and my brain keeps replaying over and over what happened when Sam walked me home after leaving Ed's flat. The memory gives me palpitations and makes my stomach do somersaults and even the pot-smoking saga at Ed's flat fades into total insignificance when I remember kissing Sam.

I had been hoping he'd give me a little kiss on the cheek and say goodnight, but I *never* expected or dreamed that he would kiss me like that. I can't get it out of my mind – it was like no other kiss ever before. I totally melted into his arms and could have stayed there all night. We kissed and kissed and in the end I had to pull away and run home panting – wracked with guilt.

Sam is so different from anyone I have ever met – nothing like any boy I knew in Cyprus – or sweet, gentle and caring Nima. Nor is he like Tom, who was also older and knew a lot about art, but still wasn't anything like Sam. Whatever it is, Sam just has an edge to him. There's no denying any more that I fancy him. There's something mysterious about him that I'm drawn to. I want to be around him, kiss him. But I don't feel entirely safe with him – not like I do with Nima. Poor Nima – he's so nice. How could I have done this to him?

That's it, I decide, that's the moral of this story. Sam is a bit dangerous and I'm infatuated with him. So maybe I should be sensible, keep my distance and stay with Nima, who is nice and *safe*. The truth is, I don't know *what* to do. And I feel terrible.

'Julia!' I hear my mother call from downstairs. 'We're back! Do you want some dinner?'

'No thanks!' I shout back and put on a cheerful nothing's wrong voice, 'I'm doing my homework and I've made myself something to eat,' I yell, hoping she will take no for an answer.

But she never does when it comes to food, so why should she do it now – especially since she's been out most of the day and probably feels she needs to check on me.

'What did you eat?' Her reply comes back, followed by, 'I'll make you some more, I'm sure whatever it was, it wasn't enough . . .'

'No really, Mama, I'm fine! I'm going to finish my homework and go to bed.'

'You can't go to bed without a proper meal. There is some moussaka in the fridge – shall I heat some up for you?'

'Oh, for God's sake,' I hear my dad interrupt. 'Leave her alone. She's not a baby – if she says she's not hungry, I'm sure it's because she is not!' Dads have their uses after all, I think with a smile.

But before I know it, Mum is standing at my bedroom door, wanting to chat. Although Greeks are not big on privacy, my mum *is* learning about it and does give me a *bit* of space. When we first came over here and we were living in a house with Anna's family, I had to share my bedroom with my brother. None of us had any privacy. My parents didn't seem to mind, but I really like having some personal space. I feel very grateful having this bedroom all to myself, even though it's small.

'So what did you do today?' she asks, perching at the edge of my bed. 'I hope you haven't been doing homework all day!'

Hmm, I muse to myself . . . You really don't want to know. I feel my face flush. 'No, I went out with Linda for a bit,' I lie, and, desperate to change the subject, I ask her about her day, knowing that my parents went to visit some new Greek friends they'd recently met and that my mum was particularly pleased to be expanding her social circle.

'They were really nice people and they have such a fabulous house,' she says excitedly. 'Almost a mansion! Honesty, Ioulia *mou*, it was huge! Six bedrooms and lots of reception rooms and a massive kitchen. They had an interior designer do it for them! It's in a place called Hadley Wood, which is almost in the countryside.' It's obvious my mum is impressed, which is saying something, because apart from the English weather, English houses were another thing the two of us hated when we first came here. Row after row of the same small old-looking houses, squashed together with no balconies or verandas or proper gardens. 'And,' she continues with renewed excitement, 'they are having a swimming pool built in the back garden! Can you imagine a garden that big in London? It's like being in Cyprus there.'

'Wow!' I say, genuinely impressed. 'A swimming pool!' I wonder when they'd get the chance to use it?

'Next time we go, you'll have to come too!' she continues enthusiastically. 'They have three children, and, one of them is a seventeen-year-old boy, who I think you would really like – he's very artistic and musical.'

Oh my God, I think to myself, is my mum trying to set me up? She'd do anything to get me mixing with Greek kids. But the last thing I need is to meet any more 'artistic' boys!

CHAPTER TEN

Girlfriends and Cousins

'So, didn't you even try a bit?' Linda asks me, stuffing a handful of crisps into her mouth during our morning break on Monday. 'Looking at you, anyone would think you've been stoned all weekend,' she carries on and gives me a little shove. Linda is her usual cheery self and looks fresh as a daisy while I look like death warmed up. The circles round my eyes are darker and deeper than usual and my head is pounding with a terrible headache from a mixture of guilt and lack of sleep.

'No, I didn't,' I tell her, giving her a shove back and helping myself to some of her crisps.

'How'd you manage that?' she says, looking inquisitively at me.

'I just said I didn't smoke and it seemed to be OK,' I reply, licking the salt off my fingers.

'So what? When the spliff got to you, you just said, "No thanks, I don't smoke" and no one said anything?'

'Not exactly . . . Sam asked me if I wanted any, seeing

54

that I don't smoke, and I said no thanks, and he said fine.'

'And then what? Every time it got passed to you, you kept saying politely, "No thanks"?'

'Actually no, Sam kept giving it to me to pass on to the next person, so nobody seemed to take any notice,' I explain, and see Scarlet walking towards us.

'Hi, you two. Do you want some chocolate?' she asks through a mouthful of the stuff. 'What are you talking about?' She breaks off some squares from the giant bar she's holding and hands them to us. 'It looks very intense.'

'You don't want to know . . .' Linda says, looking at me to gauge if I want to tell Scarlet any of this or not.

Actually, I really like Scarlet, and from the first day I met her I knew we'd get on. She is wacky and funny and a really good artist. She is definitely the only other girl in our class who loves art as much as I do. The first time we got talking, she told me she wanted to study fine art at St Martin's. I thought, wow! She is so focused. I know I want to study art, but I don't really know what or where yet, but I told Scarlet about my Saturday art classes in an attempt to show her how keen I was on art too. She thought it was cool. Her mum is a painter and has her studio in their house, and she lets Scarlet work there sometimes. Then she invited me over to see it. I thought that was so great, and that Scarlet was really friendly and generous.

Apart from Linda, Scarlet is the only other person at school I'd want to talk to about anything like this, so I quickly fill her in on the situation, although I'm surprised to find that I'm not telling either of them about kissing Sam. I guess it's the guilt. I start to wonder how many other people I'm going to end up lying to – does not telling them count as lying, or is it just being economical with the truth?

'Wow! That sounds like a *really* cool afternoon!' Scarlet says when I finish. 'Wish I was there!'

'Weren't you even tempted to try just a little bit?' Linda asks me again. 'I'm sure I would have been.'

'To tell the truth,' I say, 'I didn't like the smell very much, and also, I was just scared I would feel ill or something, or get dizzy and make a fool of myself. They were all older and they looked like they knew what they were doing and I didn't know any of them, apart from Sam, and I felt really out of place. If I did ever try any, it would have to be somewhere I feel safe and with people I know.'

'You're probably right,' Linda says thoughtfully. 'Have you ever tried it, Scarlet?'

'Yes. Well, no . . . Well, nearly. My brother smokes it all the time, so I sneaked into his room once when he was out and found half a spliff in the ashtray, so I lit it and was about to smoke it when I heard him coming back so I put it out and ran out of the room.'

'Didn't you get a chance to take a puff or anything?' Linda asked.

'Not really. I think Julia probably had more of a chance of getting stoned, breathing in all the smoke around her when she was sitting there with everyone else smoking,' Scarlet says and we all start laughing.

Suddenly my spirits lift a bit and I feel really connected with my friends. Chatting with them has helped me see the funny side of it after all my worrying. For the first time since it all happened I can laugh about it. Part of me is also dying to tell Linda and Scarlet about what happened with me and Sam, because I think they might be able to help me sort my feelings out, but I just can't bring myself to talk about it. Something is holding me back. I feel they might think badly of me because I'm seeing Nima. I just don't want to spoil the mood or risk any arguments between us. Linda is a great friend and I know she cares about me, but she really likes Ali too and Nima is his best friend so I'll keep my mouth shut and my feelings to myself until I have more time to work things out in my own head. Writing to Sophia always helps, so I decide to do that when I get home.

'Do you think Nima has ever smoked it?' asks Linda.

'I don't think so – it's not really Nima's scene. I can't imagine him ever doing anything illegal and he doesn't even smoke cigarettes,' I say and try to imagine Nima in that situation.

'What about Tony – do you think he does?'

'I have no idea, Linda, and even if he did, he wouldn't tell *me* about it,' I reply, as we start walking back to class.

The minute I get home from school that afternoon I lock

myself in my room. I have to write to my cousin Sophia and tell her all about Sam, but letters are always a risky business in our family, as our mothers still have a lot to learn about not reading other people's mail. My aunt has promised Sophia that now she is fifteen, she won't open her letters, but there is always a risk that one of her sisters might read it. Still, I'm going to take that risk because I badly need to tell Sophia everything since she's the only one I can unburden myself to.

'Dearest, darling, best cousin,' I write.

'Why are you not here? I need you and miss you so much and I wish I could talk to you instead of writing this letter, but I've got no choice. I've got so much to tell you, but you have to promise that you will destroy this letter as soon as you've read it. I don't care how you do it – eat it, burn it, cut it up into a thousand pieces, but for God's sake, DON'T leave it lying around because if anyone else reads it, I'm dead.'

Sophia and I have always been able to tell each other our innermost secrets, knowing there would always be total understanding and trust. I knew I could tell her all about Sam and the marijuana thing without her thinking that I'm a bad person or in danger of becoming a dope head or judging me. Even though we knew about all that stuff in Cyprus from school and films, I don't think we ever knew anyone who did it and certainly hadn't ever been involved with it ourselves. Our parents were always warning us against it and putting the fear of God into us, but they did that with lots of things – especially sex. 'Nice girls' don't do things like that, and as far as drugs are concerned, only drop-outs or 'really bad people' do anything of the sort. According to them, even as much as one puff of the evil weed could lead to addiction and the path to self-destruction and damnation.

I'm hoping that writing it all down for Sophia will help me to sort out my thoughts a bit.

'He is so different, Sophia. Can't put my finger on it. I never feel quite relaxed with him, which I actually find really sexy. He's a brilliant artist and a great kisser. After we left his friend's flat, he kissed me and I can't stop thinking about that kiss. It was like no other kiss I've had. So different from being with Nima. He used his tongue and everything, but he was really soft and gentle, not slobbering all over me like boys usually do and I was just sort of lost in it, Sophia mou. Even though I was really stressed out about getting home on time, we kept kissing for ages and I melted into his arms. It was brilliant. God, I'm such a two-timing bitch. How can I like him and want to kiss him and still really like Nima? But I can't help it! Honestly, Sophia, it was the best kiss ever! I keep wondering if he only did it because he'd been smoking, but whatever the reason, it was brilliant. I just have to kiss him again when he hasn't had any drugs. Oh God, just listen to me! Poor Nima, he doesn't deserve this. Why do I always seem to do this – go out with one boy and get interested in another one as well? Don't answer that . . . I think I might not like the answer.'

My mental conversation with Sophia is interrupted by

the telephone. It's Anna wanting to see how I am as she's been busy with her studies and we've not spoken for a while.

'What's been happening?' she asks, sounding a bit tired.

'Don't ask,' I reply. 'It's a long story, and I've just been writing to Sophia about it.' Anna is the only other person apart from Sophia I feel I can talk to about Sam and the thought makes me feel a bit happier.

'What have you been up to?' she says, sounding a bit perkier all of a sudden. 'What mischief have you been getting up to?'

'We'll have to meet up so I can tell you about it,' I say not wanting to go into any details in case anyone over-hears, either on her end or mine. 'When can I come over?' I ask. 'I want to have your advice and the wisdom of your older years, but most of all I want your mum to read my coffee grounds.'

'Oh, it's like that, is it?' she says mockingly, with laughter in her voice this time.

'Mmm, you've guessed it! I'm only friends with you because of your mum's spooky skills. But how are you?' I ask. 'Have you seen Peter recently?'

'That's a whole other story,' she says, and we make a date to meet up next Saturday at her house.

CHAPTER ELEVEN

The Mystic Coffee Cup

This morning, I'm actually feeling quite cheerful and alert, if a little nervous as it's the last day of term and the day of our Christmas show. The thought of standing up in front of the whole school is a bit of a worry, but the excitement of doing it is much stronger, so I put it to the back of my mind and try to listen to my dad's radio, which is also going on about Christmas and all that stuff. As it's Friday, I know that tomorrow morning I don't have to get up early because my art class has already broken up for the holidays. This thought reminds me that I won't be seeing Sam tomorrow, which makes me wonder when I'll see him next . . . I have to admit I've been hoping to hear from him all week, even though I swore not to let things with Sam go any further. Suddenly my cheerfulness has turned to gloom. Why hasn't he called me? All I've done this week is think about him and his kiss and agonise about it all and he hasn't even bothered to call. Clearly the kiss hasn't had the effect on him that it had on me.

I'm probably a terrible kisser and he's been with so many girls that kissing me is no big deal.

'What's the matter, Ioulia *mou*?' my dad enquires, sensing my sudden change of mood. 'Last day of school, remember, and then you can sleep all you want,' he says, beaming through his Father Christmas shaving foam beard.

I give him a smile and return to my hot chocolate and my thoughts.

Apart from having the best blue eyes ever, and being the best kisser *ever*, Sam also really makes me laugh. There is dry wit about his observations that I find really attractive. A couple of weeks ago I tried to explain this to Linda and she said that it's called irony. Of course I know what irony is, after all it comes from the Greek word *ironia*, so I should know, but I've never known it used the way he does. Linda says it's the best kind of English humour because it's witty.

I suppose that's what I like about Sam – his wit, his talent, his kissing and the fact that I never know what he's going to do next. But even more to the point, what am I going to do next? Since I seem to like Sam so much, does it mean I should break up with Nima?

Thank God I'm finally off to see Anna and her mum tomorrow. Just as well I didn't manage to see *Kyria* Eva sooner, because I need her more now. I hope she'll be able to throw some light on this situation and give me some clues about what I should do about all this.

* * *

'She's in her bedroom,' Anna's mum tells me cheerfully in Greek and gives us all a kiss as we enter their house. My mum has come with me, as she didn't want to miss the chance of seeing her old friend.

'Go right up, she's waiting for you.' *Kyria* Eva is grinning with obvious pleasure at seeing us, and takes my mum by the arm and leads her into the kitchen. Pushing past Stavros, Anna's brother, who blatantly ignores me, I run up the stairs to her room two steps at a time, and slam the door closed behind me.

'God! Your brother is a pain,' I moan to Anna in Greek, collapsing on the bed next to her where she is sitting cross-legged listening to music and flicking through a magazine. 'Bloody brothers, I don't know why we put up with them!'

'Why? What did he say?' she asks, putting down the magazine and giving me a hug.

'It's not what he said, it's what he *didn't* say actually,' I reply. 'Both Tony and him think they are so superior,' I carry on, rolling my eyes. Deep down I know that I'm really just a bit put out that Stavros refuses to acknowledge that finally I'm growing up and maybe I'm worth noticing. 'Your mum opened the door to us all friendly and everything, but he just stood there with not so much as a hello, his hands in his pockets at the bottom of the stairs ignoring us. It makes me feel like I'm something that got stuck to the bottom of his shoe. He's so rude!'

'Oh, just ignore him back,' Anna says, getting off the

bed to turn the music down a bit so we don't have to shout at each other. 'He's an idiot. Come on, then, tell me what's been going on before we go down to the kitchen. I'm dying to know.'

Our mums are getting the coffee ready, so I start telling Anna everything as quickly as I can. This way I won't have to explain anything in front of our mothers once her mum starts reading my cup. I hope the coffee grounds don't reveal too much and get me in trouble.

'I see,' Anna says, grinning at me with mischievous delight after I've spewed it all out. 'So, let me summarise: I don't see you for a few weeks and in that time you get yourself involved with a load of dope-head art students, end up in an opium den, do a simulated striptease for a Christmas school show, and have a marathon snogging session with a boy who is *not* your boyfriend while your mother thinks you are at home doing your homework! Bravo! You're making great progress!' she says, standing up. 'Now let's go and see what the Oracle has to say about all this . . .'

'I see a house on fire . . . lots of smoke . . . danger . . .' *Kyria* Eva says, looking intensely into my cup. We've finished our coffee and the compulsory small talk that goes with drinking it. 'You must go . . . must get out of there . . .' she continues in a spooky voice. 'No, wait . . . no, it's not a house on fire, I think it's a lantern or a candle that's burning or . . . yes, that's it . . . but there is a big cloud of smoke in the room and someone is hiding behind it. Yes, yes . . . that's it. See?' she says pointing at a swirl of brown coffee stain in my cup, which I suppose could be interpreted as smoke or cloud. 'I see two blue eyes,' she starts up again. 'Oh, Ioulia *mou*, those blue eyes again. You always have the blue eyes in your cup. You have to be careful of the evil eye – it's always blue. Someone is envious of you.' Her voice fades into a whisper, giving me the shivers.

God, that evil eye again! Greeks believe that some people have the evil eye, which means they do not have your best interests at heart. They also believe that the evil eye is motivated by envy, which is a very evil thing and can cause a lot of harm. *Kyria* Eva is always going on about it. Apparently the evil eye is usually blue or green, but since a lot of people in England have blue or green eyes, it's a bit hard to spot the evil ones. I tried to explain this to my fortune-teller, but it makes no difference. She insists that I take protective measures, which involves wearing a cross or a little blue stone on a chain. A person can get paranoid trying to protect themselves against unknown evil forces, so I let it go.

'What else do you see?' I ask wanting to get off the subject of blue eyes and with a feeling of dread of what else I might hear about them.

'There is a triangle, but it's not complete . . . and I see a road divided in two – no . . . wait . . . in three paths . . . and a big rock. That's the obstacle . . . you have to find the strength to move it . . .' she says finally, then she takes a deep breath and puts the cup down.

Wow, that was an Oscar-winning performance, I think. If she auditioned for the part of Pythia, The Sacred Oracle, *Kyria* Eva would surely get the part hands down! I take a deep breath too since I feel as if I stopped breathing for God knows how long, and I look at Anna with big eyes. We sit there exchanging looks and I feel a sense of awe. I'm convinced there is more to this than just coffee grounds. *Kyria* Eva is definitely gifted and should be on television, spooking out everyone with her readings. If I were older I'd be her agent and we could all make lots of money.

'That was interesting, wasn't it?' my mum says, looking at me and smiling inquisitively and I suddenly feel panic-stricken, wondering what on earth she must be thinking. 'Eva is obviously talking about your dilemma about what to do when you leave school.' She reaches across the table to take my hand. I stare at her blankly and think that maybe she has lost her mind.

'How's that?' I ask, and look at Anna for help.

'Well, it's obviously about your love of art, drama and writing,' she explains, looking at me lovingly, 'and the great success you had yesterday at your Christmas show, remember? Someone there must have been jealous of you doing so well. Maybe one of the girls who wished she was doing the part? Someone with blue eyes?' she continues, still making no sense at all. Yeah, right! I can't believe what she's saying. 'You know, you are torn three ways,

66

Ioulia *mou*.' She turns to look at the others as she starts to explain about the school show and everything. 'Julia is equally good at all of these subjects and she will soon have to decide which way to go when she leaves school . . .'

I can see Anna is trying as hard as I am not to laugh, but I'm also flooded with love and gratitude for my totally bonkers mother who is so naïve and nice that she would never suspect that her little girl would get herself into the situation I'm in.

My mum's only just put the key in the front door when I hear the phone ringing inside. Knowing that both my dad and brother are out, I start to panic as I'm desperate not to miss the call in case it's from Sam. I know I decided I wouldn't pursue him, but if he calls me, that's different, isn't it? Pushing past my mum I rush into the living room and grab the phone. With a sinking feeling, I realise it's not Sam but Nima and the blood rushes to my face, making me pulsate with guilt.

'Hi, babe,' he says cheerfully in his typical good-natured Nima way, 'Where've you been? I've been calling you all afternoon.'

'I went with my mum to Anna's house,' I say, and feel pleased that for once I'm not being dishonest.

'Thank God school's finished,' he says with a sigh of relief. 'Shall we meet up tomorrow? Otherwise if we carry on like this, we won't see each other till New Year's Eve.'

As I hear Nima's cheerful voice carry on, I remember

how much I like him and I miss him. 'Yes, let's meet up tomorrow,' I reply and feel happy after all that it was Nima and not Sam who called me. Nima always calms me down and makes me feel secure and happy rather than sick to my stomach and nervy. I'm really looking forward to our afternoon together tomorrow.

I hardly have time to put the receiver down when the phone starts ringing once again. I snatch it up quickly with a pounding heart, but it's just Stella, a Greek friend from my first school in London, wanting to catch up with the gossip and double-check that she is invited to Nima's party.

'You have completely forgotten me,' she complains. 'You get a boyfriend and all your old friends are history.' I know she doesn't really mean it. Stella is just as busy as I am and she's only teasing me.

'So what's been going on, Miss-Going-Out-With-Mr-Gorgeous?' she enquires, giggling. 'How's Anna and Linda and that love god of a brother of yours?'

'My brother is a pain, and Linda and Anna are fine but as far as anything else is concerned, don't ask,' I reply. 'One thing is for sure, though, Stella, there is more to life than meets the eye, and it's all in the bottom a coffee cup . . .' I say mysteriously. She laughs and calls me crazy and we promise to arrange to have a girls' day out before Christmas so we can catch up with each other.

CHAPTER TWELVE

Boy Meets Girls

'Julia,' Linda says to me thoughtfully a few days later on our way to meet Anna and Stella for our day out, 'you know it's Christmas soon?'

'Yes, I had noticed,' I say sarcastically and roll my eyes. 'What about it?'

'Well, Jewish people also have a celebration around the same time of year . . .'

'But I thought you didn't believe in Christ,' I say, gently teasing her, before she finishes her sentence.

'Yes, that's true, but if you just listen without interrupting for once,' she tells me with mock irritation, 'you might learn something new! So, as I was saying before I was so rudely interrupted, Jewish people have a festival too but it's called Hanukkah and I'd like to invite you and your parents to come to our house for a party.'

'That's nice, Linda, thank you, but what is it?' I ask, feeling curious to learn its meaning, as it was one of those words I had heard used, like leotard, but never knew what it meant. I thought Hanukkah sounded like a girl's name, and leotard I thought must be some kind of animal.

'It's the Festival of Lights and it's something to do with a miracle a long time ago about some oil that burned for eight days in a temple,' she starts explaining, but gets a bit stuck. 'I'm not absolutely sure to be honest, Julia, but it's to do with our religion. I'll ask my dad and tell you more about it.'

'OK, I'd like to know.'

'What I do know, though,' she starts up again excitedly, 'is that it goes on for eight days, a bit like your Greek Easter, and it's fun, and we have gifts and decorations and lots of food and stuff and I'd like you to come to our party. Do you think your parents would want to?'

'Don't see why not. Tell me when it is and I'll ask them,' I reply as we arrive at the entrance to the Tube where Stella and Anna are waiting.

We're going to Oxford Street which I haven't done since my shopping excursion with Nima, and we are very excited to be together again. We are all looking to buy something new to wear for Nima's New Year's Eve party, then go for a pizza in Covent Garden. Sitting on the train in a line we chat, laugh and joke loudly. Life feels good! Young, free and let loose in the metropolis with some money in our pockets. I always think of how impressed my *bapu* and my auntie Eleni would be if they could see me being able to move about so easily in one of the biggest cities in the world, getting on buses and trains, shopping with my friends, eating in restaurants and generally behaving like a sophisticated young woman. I wonder if this feeling of excitement will run out as I get older. I hope not!

Suddenly the smile freezes on my face as I look up and see Sam getting on the same carriage as us with a couple of his mates. My heart feels like it's dropped to my feet and my stomach tries to lurch itself out through my throat. Oh my God! All my thoughts and feelings from the past couple of weeks swirl in my head, making me dizzy and breathless. I pretend I haven't seen him and, feeling sick, try to carry on talking to the girls, but a few minutes later I hear Sam's deep dark voice call out to me from across the carriage.

'Hey, Julia!' he shouts and I watch him stroll across the carriage to where we are sitting.

All three of my friends turn around in amazement to look at this cool-looking boy who is addressing me.

'It's *Sam*,' I whisper to them under my breath, and before I have time to say anything else he is standing over us, smiling his sexy smile and asking lots of questions.

'How've you been, Julia? What's happening? Where you going?'

'Oh, hi Sam,' I say trying to be nonchalant and cool, 'I'm going into town, how about you?'

'Oh, nowhere in particular, just hanging out with some mates. We'll probably go to Hyde Park to listen to all the nutters at Hyde Park Corner,' he says and looks at all

71

three of my friends one at a time with his dreamy blue gaze. I have no idea what the nutters are, or Hyde Park Corner for that matter, but I just nod and try to look cheerful.

'Who are your friends?' he asks, looking back at me with a grin.

'Oh, sorry,' I say, feeling flustered, then I introduce the girls to him.

'Cool,' he says again. 'You all Greek?'

I can see Sam's magic is working on all of them. Abandoning his friends, he sits down next to Stella and starts chatting and charming everyone.

'So, Julia, is Sam coming to the New Year's Eve party?' Stella asks me with her eyes firmly fixed on Sam. I suddenly have an overwhelming desire to strangle her.

'Are you having a New Year's Eve party, Julia?' Sam asks me, looking really interested.

'Not exactly . . .' I say, frantically trying to think what I can possibly say next, when I'm rescued by one of Sam's friends calling him.

'Got to go – we change trains here,' he says, dashing off. 'Call you tomorrow, Julia,' he shouts, looking over his shoulder at me as he gets off the train.

Once the doors close behind him, I turn to Stella. 'Thank you very much!' I hiss.

'What? What did I do wrong?' she says, looking at me with big, innocent eyes.

'I wasn't planning on inviting him. It's not exactly my

party you know, and he doesn't even know Nima and probably wouldn't want to meet him either . . .' I say, my voice trailing off, realising that it's no good being cross with Stella since she doesn't know anything about Sam. We haven't seen each other for ages and I didn't get a chance to tell her about him earlier, so I start explaining a few things, leaving out the part about the kiss. 'So, you see I was definitely not planning to invite him to Nima's party,' I say, after finally filling her in on Sam.

'Sorry,' she says, sheepishly. I know what Stella's like, she wasn't trying to land me in it. She just thought he was gorgeous and got carried away.

'Oh, well,' I say, determined not to spoil the day or fall out with my friend, 'It's not your fault, I'll deal with it later.'

CHAPTER THIRTEEN

Big Fat Greek Christmas

I'm moody and sulking like a three-year-old in the back seat of my dad's car. I'm truly fed up with my parents because they are dragging me off to meet their new, rich Greek friends who are having a Christmas party. Of course Tony doesn't have to go because he doesn't have to do anything he doesn't want to. 'Tony is a young man and has his life and his friends,' my mum told me when I protested. He has his blonde, Swedish girlfriend more like, I think to myself and sulk even more. I can think of a million and one things I'd rather be doing right now instead of this. Everyone called to see if I wanted to go out today. Even Sam called to ask if I wanted to go and see an art film, but instead I have to go out with my parents! I know I made myself a promise to keep my distance from Sam but I would have liked to have the choice. Obviously as far as my parents are concerned I'm *not* a young woman, I don't have a life or any friends.

'You'll really like them, Ioulia *mou*,' my mum says for

the tenth time, turning around and smiling at me from the front seat, and annoying me even more. '*Kyria* Maria and her husband are really nice people, and their son will be there too – you know, the one who's artistic? You'll have a nice time, you'll see.'

Oh God! That's all I need, to meet another nice boy – to complete that triangle *Kyria* Eva saw in the coffee grounds and make my life even more complicated than it already is. Ignoring my mother, I let out an exasperated and exaggerated sigh and moodily carry on staring out of the window.

'Stop being such a teenager,' my dad says finally as he starts losing his patience with me. 'You used to be such a good-natured little girl.'

'It's her hormones,' my mum whispers to him as if I can't hear her.

We can see their friend's house the second we turn into their road because it's lit up like a Christmas tree, illuminating the entire street. They must have every single light turned on in every single room and it's literally pulsating with electricity. It's absolutely huge with a gravel drive and posh cars parked all along it and up the pavement. I have never seen a house like it before, apart from in some old English movies. To me it looks like a slightly shrunken-down version of Buckingham Palace, only brighter. We are greeted by a lady who is wearing an apron, and I soon realise she is not the hostess but a maid, as she helps us off with our coats. A huge, over-decorated Christmas tree sits in the hall covered in coloured fairy lights, and an elaborate chandelier hangs brightly from the ceiling. I wonder if a lot of light is a sign of wealth or if these people are just very keen to see what they are doing . . . I turn to look at my mum, who is smiling from ear to ear, and I see the person she is smiling at is an overweight lady dressed in a spangly multi-coloured party frock. She rushes towards us and gives my mum a big hug.

'Oh, *Kyria* Lea! *Kyrie* Yianni! So glad you came, so nice to see you both,' she is saying in a very loud, excited voice, and then turning around to look at me pulls me to her huge bosom, giving me big, wet, noisy kisses on both cheeks. 'And this must be Julia! Welcome to our home,' she says, releasing me, then grabbing my hand, she drags me down the hall. 'Come, I want you to meet the kids!' I look mournfully back at my mum who's glued to the same spot and is still wearing the same big smile and have no other choice but to follow *Kyria* Maria.

The kids, a whole lot of them, are all gathered together in a games room. The older boys are playing pool, while the other younger kids, boys and girls, are sprawled out on sofas and the floor watching television. The room is full of toys, games and musical instruments – including a big drum kit and a piano.

'Aaariii!' shrieks *Kyria* Maria at one of the boys in her loud, piercing voice. 'Come and meet Julia. She's the girl

I told you about. Make her feel at home and introduce her to everyone. All of you, be nice and look after her,' she demands in a combination of both Greek and English and then rushes out of the room.

'Hi Julia,' says one of the boys at the pool table in English. I suppose he must be Ari, I think, and much to my irritation, Ari is actually quite fit. I had hoped he'd be a bit of a geek so I could just dismiss him.

Ari puts his pool cue down, walks towards me with a big friendly smile and shakes my hand. He has black curly hair, chocolate-brown almond shaped eyes, broad shoulders and a strong manly handshake. 'These are my brothers and sister, and my cousins . . .' he begins obeying his mother and introducing me to everyone. 'That's Athena, my sister, over there,' he says pointing to a girl of about twelve, 'that's my brother, Andrew, and my cousin, Andy, and my other cousin, also called Ari, and that one over there is Andreas – he's just come over from Cyprus for Christmas, and that is his sister, Adriana, and their other brother, Aristoteles.

'*Yia sas,*' I greet everyone in Greek, and then wonder if I should have said my hello in English instead. They all have such Greek names and look so typically Greek that I thought I was in Cyprus for a moment.

'As you can see, our names are not very imaginative,' Ari carries on, smiling broadly. 'It does give our English friends a laugh, though. No prizes for guessing who we are all named after . . .'

'Your grandfather, who is called Aristoteles, and the other grandfather who's called Andreas?' I reply, laughing too.

'You've got it! The only one who escaped is Athena who's named after our grandmother. Is it the same in your family?'

'Oh God, yes,' I say, and recall that most of the boys from my dad's side are called Antoni, after my dad's father. 'My brother and all my boy cousins are called Tony,' I say, and we all laugh.

'So, Julia, how long have you been in England?' Ari asks me. 'My mum tells me you haven't been here long.'

'Just over a year,' I reply in Greek as I feel strange talking in English to a Greek boy. 'How about you?'

'Oh, I was born here,' he replies again in English. 'Sorry, my Greek isn't very good. I've only been to Cyprus four times and that was on holiday.'

'Really?' I say in absolute amazement, and I don't know what to say to him next. This is the first time I have met a Greek Cypriot who was actually born in England, and who doesn't speak our language. 'How come you don't speak Greek?'

'Well, I do understand quite a bit, but I just can't speak it very well. We went to Greek school on Saturdays, but it didn't really help all that much. I could speak it when I was little, but then when I started school I just forgot it.'

This is all so new to me. I find it hard to comprehend a Greek kid with such Greek parents, looking so Greek, not *speaking* Greek. Nima was born in London but he's Persian and speaks fluent Farsi.

'When I was eight my parents sent me to Cyprus to stay with my *yiayia* and *bapu* for the whole summer,' Ari explains, 'and then my Greek got really good.'

'Don't your parents speak to you in Greek?'

'Well, you heard my mum. She speaks to us in a mixture of Greek and English and so does my dad. My grandmother now lives here with us, but she doesn't speak a word of English so we have to try to speak to her in Greek somehow, but it's really hard to understand her.'

'They're useless, these English Greeks,' Andreas, Ari's cousin from Cyprus, shouts out to me in Greek from across the room in mock disapproval. 'They call themselves Greek and they don't even speak their own language.'

Much to my surprise, I find I like these Greek kids, even though I'd hoped I wouldn't so I could get back at my parents for dragging me here against my will.

'How's your English?' I ask Andreas who is around seventeen, about the same age as Ari, but somehow seems older.

'Not brilliant,' he replies, still in Greek, 'but getting better as this lot won't speak anything else.'

Just at that moment, a little old and rather frail lady dressed in black and with snow-white hair pulled off her face and rolled into a bun, walks into the room. 'Come, children, come and eat – the food is ready,' she says in Greek, in a kind, smiling voice, and beckons us to follow her. I feel almost choked up at the sight of this lovely old lady – this typical *yiayia* who looks like an older version of my own auntie Eleni. My auntie is my mother's oldest sister, who brought my mum up because their own mother died when my mum was only a baby. She is twenty years older than my mum so she brought her up alongside her own children as if she was one of them. I love my auntie Eleni like a grandmother. She is my only *yiayia*, since my dad's mum also died before I was born.

'*Entaxi, Yiayia*,' Ari says and I hear him speak Greek for the first time. 'We are coming.'

I follow her, enchanted by Ari's *yiayia*. This is the first time since being in England that I have seen a typically Greek old lady dressed in black from head to toe and it makes me feel homesick and want to give her a hug. A lot of old ladies in England are colourful and wear make-up. No matter how old they are, it seems that many of the ones I've seen have their hair permed and dyed a sort of blue or purple colour and they wear floral prints, blusher on their cheeks and pink lipstick. In Cyprus, all the old ladies I know wear black and have white hair tied up in a bun, and they look after their grandchildren and that's it.

The dining room is dazzling and all the food is lavishly laid out on a huge table. There is every kind of food imaginable on offer, and the room is decorated with balloons and streamers. Fairy lights have been placed all around the table, the picture frames, the door and window frames and up the curtains, just to give a little more illumination in case the beaming lights from the chandeliers and everywhere else were not enough!

'Come, come and eat, *mana mou*,' Ari's *yiayia* is saying to me in Greek, using a dialect I have only heard spoken in the villages in Cyprus. Calling me *mana mou* is a term of endearment to show me how much she likes me. Taking a plate from the sideboard, she starts to pile it high with food while she carries on chatting to me. Finally, she gives me the impossibly full plate and walks me back to the games room. As we walk into the room the *yiayia* starts talking to all Ari's cousins in Greek.

'It is shameful that my own grandchildren cannot speak their language,' she says to me sadly, letting out a big sigh. 'Who would have believed it that I would end up living in a foreign country, where I understand nothing and where I can't even speak to my own grandchildren!'

I feel sorry for her and think of my auntie Eleni or my *bapu* being in the same position as her at their age. It was bad enough for me when I came to England at the age of fourteen not understanding a word that was being said to me. Suddenly the feeling of loneliness and isolation I felt then comes flooding back to me through this old lady. Would she ever get to grips with a foreign language, I wonder – and would she ever feel at home in this foreign land? Somehow I can't help thinking that despite her family's success and wealth she would be so much better off in her own village with her own friends around her.

CHAPTER FOURTEEN

Festival of Lights

Unlike last year, this Christmas season seems to be full of festive gatherings and parties which my mum loves, and has also helped me keep my mind off Sam and Nima. Although I've seen Nima a few times he's been busy with his family too – some of his relatives have come over from Iran. And Sam hasn't even called since the day of Ari's party. It's just so nice to know so many more people in this country now, and feel as if we are part of something, instead of feeling like total strangers in a foreign land. Our festive gatherings last year were mainly with Anna's family and a few other Greek friends, but this year our social circle, both mine and my parents', is so much bigger.

We're getting ready for our visit to Linda's house for their Hanukkah celebration and my mum has got herself in a bit of a tizzy.

'You promise you won't leave me alone with anyone,' she says to my dad and me in a panic. 'I won't be able to talk to them. Promise you will stay with me the whole time?'

'Yes, yes,' my dad replies, mildly irritated. 'Either Julia or I will make sure you always have someone with you. Just hurry up and get ready, will you, because we are already late.'

Being late is my mum's hobby, while being early is my dad's. Going out with them together is a very stressful experience! My mum tears around getting dressed and undressed and then dressed again, looking for a suitable outfit to wear, while my dad sits, dressed and ready for hours, fretting about being late.

'I don't know why you're in such a panic,' I say to her. 'Linda's family are just like us and some of them don't speak English either.'

'Who doesn't speak English?' she asks in amazement.

'Well, Linda's grandmother or great-grandmother didn't before she died . . . which means they are used to people not speaking English, so you'll be fine. Besides, I didn't speak English when I first met Linda and she was great with me. She is very good at sign language,' I say, trying to make her laugh, but she is not amused.

Of course for me it's no surprise going to Linda's house and seeing the way they entertain, as I had been to parties there before, but for my mum it's a complete revelation.

'It's just like a Greek house!' she keeps saying to me,

mesmerised. 'Even the food is similar to ours,' she continues, looking around at the lavish dining room, the table groaning under the weight of food and drink, and the twinkling light from candles and chandeliers in every room.

'I told you, they're just like us!' I whisper in her ear, as Linda's dad is chatting away to her while I translate.

As I stand there with my mum and Linda's dad in the middle of the living room I watch the guests socialising at this happy gathering and it's like looking at a parallel culture. It's not *exactly* the same, but it is so similar that I believe anyone invited to both of the parties we've been to wouldn't be able to tell which was the Greek one and which was the Jewish one. The warm hospitality and eagerness to please their guests, the way the women are dressed, the way the men drink their whisky, and the way the children play and interact with the adults . . . it's all so similar. Also, I find listening to Linda's family speaking very interesting also because, although they speak English, they use certain words from Yiddish that I don't understand. It's almost like a different dialect, similar to the way Ari's mum speaks, in that strange mixture of Greek and English. At the end of the day, I decide, people are all the same – apart from the 'truly' English people, who are completely different and behave in their own peculiar way.

CHAPTER FIFTEEN

A New Friend

'I need to see you this afternoon, but I need to come to your house,' Nima says to me mysteriously on the phone.

This doesn't sound like Nima and I'm not sure I like the serious way he said that, so I start fretting about what he's got to tell me that is so urgent. My imagination goes into overdrive again and I start thinking perhaps he's found out about Sam.

'Why can't we meet at a café or something?' I ask him, thinking that if it is about Sam I would much rather not have the conversation at home with mum around. I've been with her all day helping with housework and I'm desperate to get away from her as she's gone into Christmas Eve mania with preparations for tomorrow.

'No, no, it's got to be at your house, I need to see you at home!' he insists excitedly, with a happy and cheerful sound to his voice this time. With great relief I put my paranoid thoughts to one side and agree for him to come over.

'OK, but can we get out for a bit, at least later?'

'Maybe, we'll see,' he answers cryptically and I put the phone down, feeling mildly anxious. What can Nima want that can't wait and has to be done here?

When the doorbell rings I'm in the bathroom putting on some lip-gloss.

'I'll get it,' my mum shouts to me from the kitchen, and then I hear her talking to Nima in her broken English on the intercom as she buzzes him upstairs.

'Julia, Julia, come quick!' my mum shouts excitedly. 'You have a guest.' As if I didn't already know.

I run downstairs to see what all the fuss is about.

'Hi, babe,' says Nima cheerfully, standing in the middle of the hall holding a big cardboard box with a big red ribbon tied in a big red bow on the top of it. 'This is for you, it's your Christmas present!'

'Wow, Nima,' I say, feeling really impressed. Instantly I feel guilty too. All I have for him is a big poster of the furry cup and saucer that I bought from the Tate when I went there with Sam, and I'm not even sure he'll like it. 'What is it?' I say again, totally intrigued.

'Open it and see,' he says, smiling from ear to ear and I reach out to take the box.

'No! Don't touch it!' he shouts and I pull back with a start. 'I'll put it on the table and then you can open it. It's OK to open a present on Christmas Eve, isn't it?' he asks, looking at my mum who is nodding approvingly.

'OK . . .' I say, feeling very confused, and follow him and my mum into the kitchen where Nima places the mystery box carefully on the table.

He grins. 'Go on then, now open it.'

I start to undo the bow gingerly, not knowing what to expect.

'You can be a bit faster than that,' Nima says and starts to help me with the knot, but then thinks better of it and lets me do it on my own.

'Hurry up, Ioulia,' my mum says impatiently in Greek. 'Let's see what's in the box.'

Finally, I untie the bow and slowly start to open the flaps at the top of the box which are held together very lightly with sticky tape. Before I have time to pull the flaps back completely, something like a jack-in-the-box, only alive, jumps up at me with a squeak, making me scream, and I leap to the other side of the room, terrified. Both Nima and my mum start laughing at me hysterically, while I stand in the corner, as pale as the moon, trying to make out what it was that leaped out at my face. Suddenly, I see it. It's the smallest, fluffiest, cutest chocolate-brown kitten I have ever set eyes on, and it's sitting beside the box on the table, looking as bewildered as I am. Oh my God! I realise Nima has got me a kitten as a Christmas present! My heart jumps for joy and I don't know who to cuddle first – him or the kitten.

'Here,' Nima says to me, as he picks up the tiny furry ball and puts it in my hands. 'Hold her, she's frightened.'

She's so small she can fit in the palm of one hand, but I hold her tenderly in both and she starts to purr. I bring my cheek to her soft fur and feel it on my face and fall totally in love with the beautiful tiny creature.

'Oh Nima, you're the best!' I say and give him a hug, being careful not to squash the kitten. 'I have been longing for a kitten since I came to England, but didn't think I'd ever be allowed to have one.'

'I asked your mum and she said it was fine,' he tells me, putting his arm around my waist. 'I know how much you miss your cat in Cyprus.'

'Thank you,' I say and give him a kiss. 'And thank you too, Mama. She is just like Chloe when I found her, only smaller . . .'

'You could call her Chloe Two,' Nima suggests, smiling.

'Oh no, Nima, there could only ever be one Chloe. But we could call her Zoë which sounds similar to Chloe. Zoë means "life" in Greek,' I explain, 'and as she seems to be so full of it, it really suits her, don't you think?'

'Brilliant!' he says, and takes her from me for a cuddle. 'So, do you want to go out for a walk or a coffee now?' He passes Zoë to my mum, who has been quietly and patiently waiting for her turn to hold her.

I look longingly at Zoë. 'I suppose we better go out just for a bit to get some food and some things for her,' I reply, not wanting to leave my new pet. 'It is Christmas Eve and I think the shops will be closing soon.'

Just as we are leaving the house my brother walks

through the door and comes face to face with my mum holding the tiny kitten in her hands stroking and cooing at it.

'Oh my God! What is that?' we hear him ask her accusingly as we run down the stairs laughing. 'Don't tell me we have to share this flat with animals now too! Keep that thing away from me or else. I just knew something like this would happen sooner or later . . .'

CHAPTER SIXTEEN

Dilemma

Zoë is curled up asleep on my pillow next to my head, making her chocolate-brown body one with my brown hair. She lay there all night and every time I woke up I could feel her little warm body beside me and I just wanted to cry with happiness. Even though it's Christmas morning and all the presents are lying unopened under the tree, and my mum has been up for ages preparing for our guests, I pretend I'm asleep so I can savour this feeling of lying with my precious, lovely new kitten for as long as possible. As I lie in my bed I think about Nima and what a truly incredible boy he is. This has to be the best present anyone has ever given me in all my life, and so thoughtful. He knows I love cats and how I miss Chloe and he went to all the trouble of getting me a kitten. I'm really lucky to have him. If Sam was my boyfriend, I wonder, would he have given me such a thoughtful present? I have no idea. The truth is, I don't really know Sam very well at all. All I know about him is that I'm attracted to him and he's exciting to be with. He likes art, yes, I know that; he's funny, yes, he makes me laugh, and yes, he kisses better than anyone; but he's cool and mysterious and doesn't give too much away. When Sam looks at me with his sparkling blue eyes I can't work out what he's thinking. When Nima looks at me with his dark brown, hot-chocolate eyes, they tell me everything.

Zoë is now purring really loudly by my left ear, but I do eventually have to break the spell and get up, as my mum is screeching for me to come and help her. I can't wait to show Zoë off to Anna and Stella who are both coming to spend Christmas Day with us.

'He is just so nice,' Stella says later, referring to Nima, while she teases Zoë with a piece of string. 'He's the perfect boyfriend! Consider yourself lucky to have someone like him – gorgeous *and* nice!' Of course this makes me feel even more guilty about my feelings for Sam.

Even though I've been thinking a lot about Sam, the fact that I haven't actually seen him lately has helped to keep my mind on Nima – although should a relationship need such effort? Even though Sam has called me a couple of times I have avoided speaking to him because I know that when I speak to him or see him I just get all confused. I also know Nima is lovely, generous, thoughtful and gorgeous, but I'm not sure I want to commit to a relationship at the age of fifteen! But I also can't handle the guilt of liking two boys at the same time . . .

'Please let me hold her now,' Anna is begging Stella, and I walk out of the room as I hear my mum call me to come and help with the table.

This is turning out to be one of the nicest Christmases I've ever had. It's almost like we are back in Cyprus, apart from the fact that it's really cold outside and we are in a flat with no backyard or veranda to sit on. I have my friends with me, and my adorable new kitten, and even though no one could replace Sophia or Chloe, I feel happy. I never thought Christmas in London could be like this. Admittedly all our guests today are Greek so this hardly makes it a typical English Christmas, but still, we're doing our best and we're definitely having fun.

'I can't wait for Nima's New Year's Eve party,' Stella says back in my bedroom after an incredible lunch. 'So what have you decided? Are you going to ask Sam or not?' she asks while she strokes Zoë who is curled up in a ball on my pillow.

'Oh God, Stella, I don't think so,' I say with a sinking feeling. 'I could do without the complication.'

'I don't see why you have to make everything so complicated,' Stella hits back with a grin. 'It's actually very simple. You take Sam and I'll have Nima – especially since your brother is still blind to my charms.' That's just typical of Stella. Give her a good-looking boy and she doesn't care – she's anybody's!

A sting of jealousy tells me I know that the problem is not that I don't want Nima or Sam, it's that I want Nima *and* Sam, and I feel too bad even to admit it to my friends. I should do the right thing and tell Sam I can't see him and that I have a perfectly lovely, gorgeous boyfriend. I need to finish with this whole liking-two-boys-at-the-same-time-game, which could end up giving me a nervous breakdown and hurting someone. Sophia's reply to my letter didn't help much either as she thought the thing with Sam sounded like great fun and very exciting. But she's not the one dealing with the guilt or being dishonest by not telling either of them about the other.

'Do you want to invite Peter?' I ask Anna, changing the subject.

'Can't decide,' she replies. 'I'm trying to cool it off with him a bit. Not that it needs much of an effort as we hardly see each other these days. Going to university will kill that relationship off anyway, so I might as well just get used to it.'

I can't believe how things have changed since last year for the two of us. Anna couldn't wait for any opportunity to be with Peter and the thought of going away to uni and leaving him behind used to plunge her into a black mood, and *my* biggest problem was learning to speak English so I could actually have a conversation with a boy.

'Anyway, you might meet someone new at the party,' Stella says cheerfully and jumps off the bed to go and see what is happening in the other room. The parents and all the adults have started singing in their usual way and someone is playing the guitar. There is never a Greek gathering without singing and dancing. Card-playing is also a big thing for Greek adults; often it's planned in advance and guests are invited for dinner and then a game of cards. The singing thing, however, just happens spontaneously at any gathering where there is food and drink. It's part of our culture and even if we teenagers moan at the inevitability of it, we all join in and love it really, and we'd miss it if it didn't happen.

'Come on, girls,' Stella's mum is calling us from the other room. 'We need your tuneful voices here.'

'Let's go. I can hear Tony and Stavros singing,' Stella says and gives me a wink. 'I need to do some harmonies with your brother.'

CHAPTER SEVENTEEN

New Year's Resolution

The new year is fast approaching – only an hour to go – and Nima's party is in full swing. The lights are down, the music is loud and everyone is in high spirits.

This last week leading up to the party has been full of excitement for all of us, and Linda and I have done nothing else but talk about it. We had so much to organise what with working out our wardrobe and what we were going to do with our hair, nails and make-up, we haven't had time for anything else. Also, the intoxication of helping to organise a party and being the owner and carer of a beautiful, gorgeous little kitty-cat has luckily left me with precious little time to think about Sam or any of that stuff . . . Instead I have been spending a lot of time with Nima, Ali and Linda, either at my house playing with Zoë – although the boys soon got fed up with that – or at Nima's, getting his house ready for the party.

We moved the furniture about, sorted out the lighting, put up decorations, and Ali and Nima got some great music together for the night. It was really good fun doing it all together and feeling happy instead of stressed out for a change. It felt like it used to be before I met Sam. Nima, thank God, liked his Christmas present and stuck it up on his bedroom wall. It felt good explaining what I knew about the surrealist movement, and I telling him about going to the Tate with Sam and his friends. Nima seemed impressed that I knew so much about art and I was pleased he didn't make anything of me going to an exhibition with another boy.

But now that the party is in full flow, I'm exhausted and my feet are killing me. I have been looking forward to Nima's New Year's Eve party for so long, even though I knew it wouldn't be anything like the parties I was used to, and now I'm not so sure if it's not a bit of an anticlimax. New Year's Eve is a very big deal in Cyprus. Easter Sunday is the number one celebration of the year when it comes to partying and having fun, and New Year's Eve the second. It's about new beginnings, and the promise of what's to come. It's about letting go of the old and welcoming in the new with all the anticipations and expectations that the new year holds. The night is always full of hope and has a magical hold on people.

Ever since I can remember, there has never been a New Year's Eve when we didn't have a party and a family gathering. My aunts and uncles and family would take turns each year to host a party in their house, which would start in the early evening and go on until well after midnight. There was never any question whether children, no matter how old or young they were, would be included. When we were very young we would fall asleep in our mother's arms and then, when we were older, we would try to stay awake till after midnight before collapsing. By the time we were nine or ten we were able to join in with the real fun, which would start after we saw the new year in. There was the inevitable singing and dancing, but, most importantly, the card games. Playing cards on New Year's Eve is a tradition in most Greek homes and the joy of winning money off the grown-ups was always immeasurable.

Even though I wasn't going to be with my family for the first time ever, I was really excited about tonight and wanted to be with Nima and to have fun at a party without parents and brothers. But I have been on my feet for hours. All I've done so far tonight is run around making sure no one stubs out their cigarettes on Nima's mother's Persian carpets or throws up in the flowerpots. Foolishly, I promised her that I would be personally responsible if anything gets trashed, so I've been totally stressed out. My faithful friends are too busy dancing – or, in Linda's case, snogging Ali and making up for lost time at last – to help me in any way. I haven't even spent any time with Nima as he is doing his share of stressing out too.

When I finally find five minutes to sit down for a little rest, I kick off my new high-heeled shoes and rub my aching feet. I decide that being the co-host of a party is not worth it. In fact, I'm now totally convinced that going to other people's parties is hugely preferable. I will never again let anyone talk me into having a party of my own or helping out at someone else's. Oh well, I think stoically, one more thing I have learned for future reference.

I hardly have time to start to enjoy my little rest and a sip of cider when I hear Stella squealing and calling my name from the other side of the room.

'Julia, quick, come here!' she is shouting. 'Look who's here.' She points to the door.

Luckily I have already put my glass down on the table when I look up to see who has arrived, or I would surely have dropped it all over Nima's mother's precious carpet, along with the pit of my stomach and my jaw. Standing in the doorway to the living room I see Sam, with his mate, Ed, and Ed's girlfriend, Laura. I haven't seen Ed and Laura since the Tate Gallery and pot-smoking saga. I quickly look away, hoping desperately that when I look back they'll all have disappeared and just have been figments of my over-stressed imagination, but unfortunately they are all as real as Stella grinning at me from across the room. Bloody hell, I think, what are they doing here – and how did they know where the party was?

'Hi, Julia!' Sam shouts from across the room in his usual way, as if it's the most natural thing in the world just to arrive at someone's party totally uninvited and bring some of your totally uninvited mates along too.

'H-H-Hi,' I stutter, but can't even hear myself talk. Walking across the room, cool as can be and followed by Ed and Laura, Sam comes over, takes me in his arms, and gives me one of his dreamy kisses which sends me into a spin and nearly makes my legs buckle beneath me.

'Cool party,' he shouts over the loud music, as he releases me from his grip. 'I bumped into your friend Stella in the high street just after Christmas and she told me about it.' He carries on, oblivious to the fact that I'm standing dumbstruck about to have a nervous breakdown while I scan the room to see if Nima is anywhere to be seen. Luckily I can't see him. Ali's too busy snogging Linda to have noticed anything, and hopefully nobody else in their gang saw anything.

'Whose place is this?' he asks.

'Can we get a drink?' Ed butts in.

'It's Nima's house,' I mumble, ignoring Ed.

'Who's Nima?' asks Sam.

'My boyfriend,' I reply, barely audible.

'Oh yeah, right, cool . . . didn't know you had a boyfriend, but maybe you said. Can't remember. Is he here?'

'Well, yes, it *is* his house,' I say now a bit louder, trying to regain my composure. I seem to have gone into a daze and I can't formulate any useful thoughts – until I suddenly get a glimpse of Nima across the room which shocks me back to life and into a state of complete panic.

I feel as if the sweat is pouring off my face, which I'm sure is doing nothing for my carefully applied make-up or my complexion. This is all Stella's fault, I think, and dart her a look that could instantly kill. Why does she have to be such a pain and mix everything up? Why couldn't she just stay being obsessed with my brother? Why didn't she at least tell me she'd asked Sam? A right fine mess this is and I can't cope with it.

Just as I'm about to start hyperventilating she walks up to us, all smiles and flapping eyelashes, oblivious to my murderous intent.

'It's nearly midnight, Julia,' she says, 'we all need to have a drink and Sam doesn't have one. Would you like a drink, Sam?' she asks him and I can't bring myself to even look at her, I'm so angry with her.

'That would be great, thanks,' he says, seemingly unaware that there is anything wrong.

'Come with me and I'll get you one,' she says, taking him by the hand and leading him towards the kitchen, the others following behind.

Although I'm really, really cross with Stella I also know that strictly speaking it's not her fault that I'm in this mess as she has no idea exactly how much I like Sam. Anna and Sophia know, and even Linda has an idea, but I haven't told Stella everything. As much as I like Stella, we don't really see much of each other these days, which makes it awkward to feel comfortable sharing my feelings about my dilemma. She's fun to be with, but I don't know if I could really trust her not to spill my secrets. The only reason I hadn't told Linda about the kissing session with Sam is because I didn't want her to tell me off or feel disloyal to Nima since we are all such good mates. At the moment it's enough that I can talk it through with Anna and Sophia.

'Hi babe, there you are!' Nima joins me and puts an arm around my waist. 'Haven't seen you all night – are you OK? Who was that guy you were talking to just now? Haven't seen him before.'

'Oh, he's a friend of mine from my art class,' I say, trying to sound cool and indifferent and hoping that Nima didn't see Sam kiss me.

'Didn't know you invited him,' he says a bit surprised, but he doesn't mention anything about the kiss.

'Actually, Nima, I didn't invite him, Stella did,' I tell him apologetically.

'Does Stella go to your art class too?' he asks sounding confused.

'No, she just knows him.'

'She probably fancies him, knowing Stella,' he says with a grin. 'He's a cool-looking guy.'

'Yeah, you're probably right,' I say, trying not to think about Stella and Sam together, and we start dancing with the others, even if my heart is pounding and my feet are still killing me.

In spite of myself, I'm soon starting to enjoy the party. I

am reminded again just how sweet and lovely Nima is and how much I really care for him.

The trouble is that Sam just does something to me. When I'm with him I get all stirred up and I just don't know what to do about it. I so wish he wasn't here. Stella has a lot to answer for. I can see her across the room now dancing with Sam, wrapped around him, oozing charm and trying to be sexier than sexy with her micro-skirt practically up around her waist. Part of me thinks she's welcome to have him. But another part of me still wants him for myself.

Nima is holding me really tight now and starts to kiss me, but all I can think about is that I wish I was kissing Sam. Nima's kiss is sweet and tender and I'm really fond of him, but it just doesn't do what Sam's kiss did to me. Why? Why do I feel like this? I have this gorgeous boy who is so nice and good-looking and everyone wants to go out with him and I'm lusting after someone who is trouble more than anything else. It just doesn't make any sense . . . I'm always reading in magazines about *chemistry* between two people. Is that what I have with Sam? *Chemistry*? I'm so confused.

I can't believe I feel like this. I try hard to get a grip, but I'm totally churned up and can't focus on being happy, dancing with – or kissing – Nima. This party was the main reason I didn't go to Cyprus over the Christmas holidays. But now I'm beginning to think it would have been better if I had gone.

Nima clearly starts to sense that I'm holding back and wonders what is wrong with me. 'Are you OK?' he asks.

'Yes, yes. I'm fine, thanks. Just a bit tired,' I say, trying not to look at Stella and Sam. Instead I turn round to look at Linda and Ali who are also wrapped around each other on the dance floor.

'Finally!' I say to Nima in an effort to sound normal. 'At last Ali and Linda have got it together.' Just at that point someone starts yelling and flashing the lights on and off.

'It's nearly midnight,' Nima says, squeezing my hand, and everybody starts the countdown.

In Cyprus, this would be the moment, before all the hugging and kissing, where we all sing a special New Year's Eve song which always makes me cry. It's a bittersweet song about letting go of the old, despite the sorrow that separation might bring, and allowing in the new, which will bring joy and happiness. Unlike most people, I have always found the song deeply sad. I never understood why you have to let go. Surely all the things that happened last year are good too and you don't have to put the poor old year in the dustbin just because a new one has come along? I am suddenly engulfed by an overwhelming feeling of nostalgia and melancholy and can't believe I'm spending a New Year's Eve away from my family. Everyone else is cheering now, and kissing one another and generally making lots of noise. I think of my cousin Sophia and wish I was with her. But Nima gives me a hug and kisses me on the lips.

'Happy New Year, Julia,' he says sweetly. He looks at me so lovingly, and I look at his beautiful face and suddenly burst into tears. Nima looks at me in bewilderment. I give him a huge hug and promise myself that I will be good.

CHAPTER EIGHTEEN

Double Trouble

It's the first of January, and I'm lying in bed under my duvet, cuddling Zoë and feeling very sorry for myself. A new year has now begun and I'm supposed to be feeling happy and full of joy for what the year ahead promises. Instead, I'm totally depressed. The events from last night's party have left me feeling like that bittersweet song, but mostly *bitter* at the moment. I know it's all my fault, but I just can't shake off this gloomy cloud that's hanging over me. Honestly, I can't believe that I'm feeling this way over two boys. Last year I had much more to be depressed about – the English weather, being homesick, the fact that I didn't know that many people . . . And, even if I'd had lots of friends then, I wouldn't have been able to speak to them properly. And now, just look at me! I have lots of lovely friends, I can communicate with them perfectly well, yet I'm miserable as hell. It's so stupid!

I could have gone home to Cyprus for Christmas and New Year to see my old friends and the rest of my family, but instead I stayed in London for a boy – and ended up agonising over *two* of them . . . What a sap I am. This goes against all my principles. Like I always said to Sophia, boys are great, but they are not the centre of the universe and we cannot allow them to hold the key to our happiness. Obviously, I need to take some of my own advice!

With that thought, I jump out of bed and start writing a letter to Sophia. Writing down my thoughts to my cousin seems to be the only way I can make sense of my feelings. Talking to Anna is also great but talking to Sophia is what I've always done since I was really small and it's the best way to help me put things into perspective – although this might have something to do with the fact that there is no one to talk back and confuse matters (until she sends me a reply!). Sitting at my desk, wrapped up in my duvet and with Zoë curled up on my lap, I start to write.

'Oh God, Sophia mou, I have made a complete mess of everything . . . I suppose I should decide who I like most and choose between Nima and Sam. The trouble is I like them both for different reasons and I don't want to give either of them up. That, of course, is assuming that either of them still want me . . . I wouldn't blame them if they don't, since I'm such a basket case. Ideally what I'd like is to have two boyfriends. I'm trying to like just being with Nima, but it's hard. It's like I love and adore you, but why can't I love Anna, and Linda too? Why does it have to be exclusive? I know I'm being selfish and *only thinking about myself, but I also definitely don't want to hurt Nima. I like him too much. That's what's making me agonise about it all so much. I do know that I have to make a choice eventually . . .'*

This letter is like a *déjà vu*. A year ago I was writing to her about making a choice between Tom and Nima. Perhaps I'm destined always to like two boys at the same time and to forever be two-timing everyone I go out with, but last year it was somehow easier to make the decision. I just knew Tom was wrong for me. But this situation is harder. Oh God, I wish I didn't like either of them.

'Maybe I should just forget them both, instead of trying to have them both. Much less complicated . . .'

As I write, I have a flashback from last night's party, and it occurs to me that this dilemma might not be a problem for much longer. The way Stella and Sam were carrying on with each other on the dance floor might put me totally out of the picture anyway. But instead of easing the pressure, that thought just makes me feel even more depressed. Does Sam like Stella now?

Stella seemed to be doing most of the flirting last night with Sam, but it's not as if I noticed him doing much resisting. Of course I know I shouldn't have any reason to be upset or jealous, as he's *not* my boyfriend. Even so, just the thought of Stella receiving one of Sam's dreamy kisses makes me shudder and feel sick to my stomach.

'It all seemed so much easier in Cyprus,' I start writing again, desperately trying not to think about Stella and

Sam together. '*But then again, we were both so much younger and so were the boys we went out with. Maybe I will never be able to fit in here. Maybe I'll never be happy with just one boy no matter where I am . . .*'

CHAPTER NINETEEN

Going Greek

The unwelcome sound of the telephone echoes across the flat disturbing the morning peace, and for once, I wish it would shut up. Ignoring it, I carry on writing and hoping someone else will pick it up. I know it won't be Tony as he'll still be sleeping off the effects of last night. I heard him come home from his New Year's Eve party around seven a.m. so I guess we won't be seeing much of him today.

When the phone is eventually picked up, I hear my mum talking in a hushed voice to somebody. I don't even care who it is. Then all of a sudden I have an overwhelming desire to be with my mum, even though I don't want to talk about any of my troubles to her. I just want to sit with her and be comforted and feel like a little girl again with no boys to worry about.

'*Kalimera* Mama, *kali hronia*,' I say wishing her a good morning and a Happy New Year as I walk into the kitchen in my pyjamas, cradling Zoë in my arms.

'*Kali hronia*, Ioulia *mou*,' my mum says, rushing over to me and wrapping me up in her arms, kissing me loudly on both cheeks and gently smoothing my hair off my face. 'I can't believe you are awake! We tried to ring you last night at midnight, but no one was picking up at Nima's house. How was the party?'

'Fine,' I say quickly, and add, to change the subject, 'Who was that on the phone?'

'It was *Kyria* Maria, wishing us Happy New Year and inviting us over to their house this evening. So, tell me about the party,' she says, all smiles.

Luckily, before I have a chance to respond, my dad walks in and gives me a big hug too.

'*Hronia Polla, kai kali hronia*, Ioulia *mou*,' he says too in the customary seasonal greeting, wishing me a long life and a happy new year ahead.

A long, happy, two-timing life, I think to myself. Perhaps I should have been born a sultan in some ancient time and then I could have had a harem. And anyway, why shouldn't women have harems? For the first time in hours, I feel a smile creep on to my face.

'Sit down, and tell me all about your New Year's Eve,' my mum says, not letting go of the subject. She starts to warm up the milk for my hot chocolate.

Realising I will have to tell her something, I sit down at the kitchen table to watch her make my breakfast. 'It was fine, Mama,' I say, deciding to shake off my mood. 'But it was hard work. And one thing is for sure: I never want to have a party like that, you will be relieved to hear. I also missed not being with all of you. It was strange not singing our New Year song, and I missed Sophia too.'

'We missed you too, Ioulia *mou*, but it must have been nice being with your friends. You probably would have missed them more if you were with us,' she says with a smile, handing me the steaming cup of hot chocolate. 'What about Nima, did he enjoy it?'

'I'm not sure. It was hard work for him too, and he probably never wants to have another party ever again either . . .'

'Never mind, you can have a nice time tonight with us,' she says cheerfully. 'We are going to Ari's parents and they said to bring you along as all the kids will be there too. You had a good time there last time, didn't you?'

'It was OK . . .' I say a bit reluctantly at first, and then decide that it probably isn't such a bad idea to be with some Greeks for a change. Since writing to Sophia this morning, and missing a Greek-style New Year's party last night, I'm starting to wonder if all my problems and dilemmas are down to cultural differences. I keep thinking if I was going out with a Greek boy there would be less room for misunderstanding and complications since our backgrounds would be the same. To be honest, I think I might be kidding myself, but maybe it's worth getting to know this Greek crowd and see where it takes me.

Like the last time we were here, Ari's house is doing a

great job at imitating a lighting shop – only this time it's not just pulsating with lights, it's also pulsating with very loud Greek music. I can't imagine what their neighbours must be thinking, and I can see from the expression on my parents' faces that it's not exactly their idea of fun.

'I hope someone turns the volume down soon or I'll go home deaf,' my dad complains.

'It's probably the kids,' my mum tells him hopefully but looks worried.

I think it sounds great! I haven't heard Greek music amplified like this for over a year – not since the last party I went to with Sophia before I left Cyprus. I can't wait to go in.

'So pleased you came too, Julia,' Ari's mum shouts over the noise as we make our way in. 'The kids are in the games room. They are having their own party. Go and find them – they're expecting you.' Then she takes my parents off to another part of the house where the grown-ups are going to play cards. I hope for my sake it's quieter over there or we'll be leaving the party sooner than I'd like.

Following the music, I make my way to the games room to look for Ari, who, as soon as he sees me, stops dancing and runs over to welcome me with a big hearty hand-shake.

'Glad you could come, Julia,' he shouts over the music. He puts a strong arm around my shoulders and leads me over to a table which has been converted into a bar with mostly soft drinks and some cider and lager. 'I was going to call and invite you tonight, but my mum said she'd already spoken to your mum and said you were coming. What would you like to drink?'

While Ari's getting me some cider I look around the room, which I'm glad to see is a lot less illuminated than the rest of the house. Some of the faces in the room I remember from last time, but there are none of the little kids, just the older cousins this time and some more people I've not seen before.

Everyone is dancing the *Tsiftedeli,* which is a sort of Greek belly dance that involves lots of gyrating the hips and jiggling about. It looks very sexy and is great fun. As it's quite a feminine dance, it's brilliant for the girls, but boys always join in too, and I'm really amazed how good these Greek–English boys and girls are at doing this dance. They're all singing along and seem to know all the words, even if most of them hardly speak any Greek and some of them have only ever been to Cyprus a couple of times. I wonder if dancing like that is in your blood, but it seems strange to me if most of them were born in England and know so little about the place the music comes from. These kids are as Greek as I am, only it's a different kind of Greekness. I think it's about the cultural identity that my dad was talking to me about after we went to Linda's Hannukah party. 'People like to belong,' my dad had said, after we came home from Linda's. 'Everyone needs an ethnic identity and when you are away from your country you look for ways to hang on to your roots.'

'Sorry, Julia, I've been rude, I should have introduced you to more people,' Ari says, as he sees me scanning the room. He hands me a glass of cider. 'I forgot you don't know everyone.'

'No, don't worry, Ari,' I say, dreading the thought of being introduced to all these people, as there are so many of them. But then if most of them are family and have the same name, I should be fine, I think and smile to myself.

The music is intoxicating and suddenly I'm totally immersed in the sound of my Greek culture. Any thoughts of Sam or Nima seem a thousand miles away and all I want to do is dance. Ari reads my mind and pulls me into the middle of the dance floor and we start to move and gyrate sensually along with everyone else. The beat of the drums, the sound of the bouzouki and the familiar song lyrics send me into a trance and I'm lost in the rhythm of the music which I know as well as I know my own heartbeat.

CHAPTER TWENTY

Tasting the Pollen

'Well, I thought that was a very nice party last night,' my mum says to me the next day. I'm sitting in my pyjamas at the kitchen table, having another very late breakfast, and trying not to be irritated by the parental interrogation about how the evening went with Ari and all the other Greek kids. It's two in the afternoon, and I have finally caught up with all the sleep I've lost in the last forty-eight hours. My mum is dying to know how I got on but I just don't feel like talking about it with her.

After we got home from the party, I went straight to bed and lay there, head still spinning and pulsating with the sound of the music and the sensation of Ari's hand on my hip while we danced. Gloriously exhausted, I drifted into the best sleep I'd had for days.

'You seemed to really enjoy yourself last night, with all that dancing,' Mum carries on.

'Yesss, Mama, I did,' I groan through a mouthful of yogurt and honey.

'And Ari seems like a very nice boy, you both seem to get on really well,' she says, pushing her luck with me just that bit further.

'*Yesss*, Mama, we do,' I say. It would be so much nicer if I could enjoy the memory of last night without having to talk over the details with my mother. I shove another spoonful in my already full mouth to avoid saying something I might regret, as I know she means well.

'You know, Ioulia *mou*,' my mother continues in a soft, confiding voice as she reaches out to pat my hand. 'I know you are going out with Nima, but you are only fifteen. At this time in your life, you are like a beautiful butterfly and you have to taste all the pollen around. You have to fly from flower to flower and be free. Do you understand what I'm saying?'

I stop eating and look at my mother with a stupefied expression on my face. Oh my good God! I can't believe what I'm hearing! And here I was thinking it was just the same old attempt at parent–teen communication. I don't know whether to burst out laughing or be shocked, so I just sit there and keep staring at her. Is my mother advising me to two-time with her hilarious metaphor? Well, what do you know. Even my mother thinks it's OK to have two boyfriends! Or maybe even three?

'Ari is a nice boy,' she carries on, oblivious to my stunned reaction. 'You can go out with him sometime if you want, to the cinema or something, with some other boys and girls – you know, get to know each other . . . He's a good boy, with a nice family, *and* he's Greek!'

I suppose my mum does have a point, I think while I'm getting dressed to go and visit Anna. I suppose in a way I'm only doing what she said, 'tasting the pollen', metaphorically speaking. No good getting too hung up over one boy. The only trouble is, instead of getting hung up over one boy, I seem to be getting hung up over two, and, judging from the way I feel after last night, it's rapidly becoming three.

I'm desperate to see Anna, sit in her bedroom, just the two of us, listen to all our favourite Greek music and talk. Anna's the best person after Sophia to really talk to, even if she is a bit grown-up about things sometimes. Thank God she is like that, though, because if all my friends were as immature as Stella, I'd be in real trouble. Talking of Stella, I can't bring myself to speak to her at the moment as I'm still furious with her. I don't know what I'm more cross with her about – poking her nose in where it wasn't welcome, or possibly snogging Sam. I haven't had a chance to speak to any of my friends since the party and I can't wait to find out the gossip, and how Anna got on. I haven't been a very good friend lately. I've been totally self-absorbed with all my dramas, and forgetting that my friends have some dramas of their own.

I blame my rampant hormones and my butterfly wings!

'The way I see it, Julia,' Anna says to me with mock disapproval, sitting cross-legged on the bedroom floor

117

while I lie on the bed, 'is that you are just plain greedy . . . Why can't you be satisfied with just one nice boyfriend like everyone else? Why do you need three?'

I laugh and throw a pillow at her.

'Joking apart, though,' she adds, her voice suddenly taking a serious tone, 'you have to do something about all this. How would you like it if Nima was seeing two other girls at the same time as you?'

I'm not sure how to answer Anna's question at first. I hadn't really considered things that way round. All I've been concerned with is making sure Nima wouldn't find out about how confused I am about my feelings for him and for Sam, but I never considered how I would feel if it was the other way round.

'I guess,' I say after a few minutes' thought, 'I wouldn't mind how many girls Sam goes out with – even though I feel pretty sick about him maybe snogging Stella, but I think that's just because it's Stella . . . and Ari might have a girlfriend anyway for all I know, and I wouldn't really care. But you might have a point about Nima. It's different with him . . . I suppose I would mind if I found out he was going out with someone else behind my back, but then that's just hypocritical of me isn't it? If Nima liked another girl as well as me and he told me and we talked about it, then . . . I'm not sure, but I think I would try to understand. I mean, we are not married or anything – and look how I'm carrying on.'

'So what are you going to do about it?' Anna says

looking at me straight in the eyes. 'Are you going to tell him?'

'I don't know yet,' I say. I have no idea how to handle this – and besides, I'm not actually going out with anyone else . . . 'What I do know, though, is that I don't actually want three boyfriends. I don't mind having the one official boyfriend, and the other two, well . . . one for the occasional snogging and the other for dancing with. What's so wrong with that?' I add, but I know perfectly well that I'm deluding myself.

'Maybe you should stop being infatuated with the other two and just concentrate on the one?' Anna suggests.

'I don't want to *concentrate* on anyone,' I tell her, 'I just want it to be easy and to have *fun*. Isn't that what we are supposed to do at our age?'

CHAPTER TWENTY-ONE

Girl Power

I never thought I'd ever see the day I was actually glad to be back at school. After all the tribulations of the Christmas break, I'm glad of anything that will take my mind off my dilemmas, even if it is the boring Miss Jones and her sorry attempts to teach us how to cook. She has no idea about food. Not that I'm an award-winning chef myself or anything, but teaching us how to make mashed potatoes? Honestly, it's an insult to the intelligence of any self-respecting fifteen-year-old.

'Why can't they give us some rubber gloves to wash up with?' Linda complains while we delve into the soapy water at Miss Jones's instruction.

'This is doing nothing for my soft-as-a-baby's-bottom hands – they are rapidly turning into shrivelled-as-Miss-Jones's-face,' she carries on, and we start giggling in our usual juvenile way. I had forgotten how much fun it was being with Linda at school.

It's nice to escape from boy troubles for a while. All

these intense and conflicting feelings about them have taken up so much of my emotional energy, not to mention probably boring my friends to tears. I've decided to cool it with all of them for a bit, although it's hard to cool off too much with Nima without going into too many explanations as he *is* my official boyfriend. I did however manage to keep Sam at bay for the last few days of the holidays by not answering the phone, in case it was him. I can't face talking to him at the moment. Apart from making a New Year's resolution to be good, I know I wouldn't be able to resist asking about Stella and I don't know how to approach it. I know I'll be seeing him soon at art class, but I'm putting it off till then.

Still, I had a really nice time for the rest of the holidays. Linda seems to be in new romance bliss with Ali at the moment and, since Ali is Nima's best friend, the four of us hung out together a lot. Without Sam around to distract me, time spent with Nima and my friends was nice and easy and really fun. So much nicer than feeling all churned up and gloomy about everything.

'Come on, girls, get your bowls ready,' Miss Jones screeches at us across the room, as she prepares to do her quality control inspection of our mashed potatoes. Honestly is this the rational behaviour of a grown woman?

'Rubbish! Full of lumps,' she shouts at Scarlet. 'What do you call this? Disgusting . . . that's what I call it.' She carries on berating the poor girl. Anyone would think the place was on fire with all the fuss she's making. There is definitely a sadistic streak in Miss Jones's character – probably due to the fact that she is a hundred and five and still a Miss. And anyway, so what if Scarlet can't make smooth mashed potatoes? She is a brilliant artist and I think that's a hundred times more important! I look over at her to give her some reassurance, but she seems to be completely unfazed by all the shouting.

'Have you nothing to say, young lady?' Miss Jones says to Scarlet. 'You will do this again till you get it right.'

Scarlet carries on staring and not saying anything until Miss Jones finally moves on. Scarlet is so funny. She really knows how to get the teachers going – she doesn't do it to everybody, only the teachers who seem to pick on her with no real reason – and it's great to see them get really wound up while she remains cool and unflustered. Sometimes I wish I could be that calm and collected, instead of always feeling like I'm on an emotional roller-coaster!

CHAPTER TWENTY-TWO

Flattery Always Works

It's my first Saturday back at art class and I'm really nervous about seeing Sam again. Even though he now knows I'm going out with Nima he still called me a few times during the holidays which goes to prove that either Sam doesn't care that I have a boyfriend or he just wants us to be friends. That's what I mean about Sam – I never know what he might be thinking. Whilst I managed to avoid his phone calls, I didn't manage to avoid an interrogation from my brother who kept answering the phone.

'Ring all your boyfriends and tell them not to call here,' Tony shouted at me after the second time Sam called during the holidays. 'This is the last time I'm going to lie on your behalf!'

My brother is such a pompous git sometimes, but I really wanted to keep the promise I made myself to stay away from Sam for a while, and not answering the phone was the only option I could think of.

The second I see Sam across the room my knees start to wobble. I chat to some people sitting around me, pretending I haven't seen him, but of course as soon as he sees *me*, he swaggers across the room to say hello in his usual laid-back, everything's-cool Sam way. The thing I'm realising about Sam is that he's just *too* easygoing. You just can't tell what he's feeling because he always looks cool and composed and never gets flustered, unlike me, who gets all knotted up about everything.

'Hey, Julia, how you doing? Where've you been? Come and sit here,' he says. I walk over tentatively. 'Have you been away? I tried calling you a couple of times to meet up. I think I spoke to your dad or your brother,' he carries on, and I'm grateful he's not giving me the chance to say anything back. 'Was the rest of your holiday good?'

'Yes, thanks,' I manage to say, finally regaining the power of speech, 'but I had loads of homework to do . . . you?'

Before Sam can reply, the teacher demands our attention.

All through the lesson I keep trying to work out how I'm feeling (besides sick with nerves) about seeing Sam again, and I keep stealing sidelong glances at him. I was really quite good at keeping my mind on Nima when Sam wasn't around, but with that one gesture of asking me to sit beside him, he has cast his spell on me again. That's the only way I can describe the way I feel about Sam – spellbound. I'm sure *Kyria* Eva would have something to say about this if she looked into my coffee grounds. He is such a mysterious and attractive personality, not to mention just gorgeous to look at and perfect to kiss. Brushing away the memory of him and Stella, I keep glancing at his lips, wishing he would attach them to mine again.

'Fancy a cup of coffee before going home?' Sam asks me on the way to the bus stop after the class. I can't help but say yes. I just love being with him. Also, I decide this could be a good opportunity to find out about him and Stella. Even though I've been dying to find out what's been going on between them, I haven't asked Stella as she hasn't called. She must know she crossed the line asking Sam to the party and is feeling too guilty to speak to me. But I'm not going to call her. I really think *she* should be calling *me* to apologise.

At the coffee house, Sam stirs his cappuccino and stares straight into my eyes. 'Julia,' he says in his gravelly voice.

Oh my God, I think, and I start to heat up. He's going to ask me something deep and meaningful. I hold my breath . . .

'Would you be into doing some modelling for me?'

WHAT? That's definitely not what I expected to hear. What kind of question is *that*? I feel vaguely confused and disappointed. I'd worked myself up to hearing something more like: 'How's your boyfriend, and are you still going

125

out with him, and do you still want to snog me?' or even: 'How's your sexy friend Stella?', which I probably wouldn't want to hear, but would still be more appropriate than, 'Would you be into doing some modelling for me?' That's just typical of Sam, keep it on a practical level and don't get personal or emotional.

'What *sort* of modelling?' I eventually ask and feel myself getting flustered.

'You know, pose for me.'

'What, like a photographic modelling sort of thing, you mean . . . ?' I say, trying to sound cool, composed and trying to remember if Sam ever said he was into photography, while inside me everything is wobbling.

'No, I mean like a life drawing modelling sort of thing,' he says with a laugh. 'All this still life crap is really boring, and I've done it so many times. There are no life drawing classes here yet and it's really what I want to be doing. I've done it a few times before and I really prefer it, but it's hard finding good models.'

'What do I have to do?' I ask, starting to feel flattered that Sam thinks I might be a good model, even if my face has broken out into red blotches by now from embarrassment.

'Nothing. Just sit there and let me draw you. I can sit for you too if you want to try life drawing.'

I have never thought of life drawing as an option. I'm always doing fashion drawings, or girls' faces either from imagination or magazines, but drawing someone who would sit professionally for me, let alone a boy, has never even crossed my mind. As I watch Sam chatting to me across the table I realise that despite the kissing and the marijuana smoking, the hanging out together and the sexual tension between us, Sam treats me like a friend. He's totally cool about our friendship and doesn't seem to be at all churned up about anything, unlike me. He's friendly and nice and normal, and again unlike me, not interested in talking things over or analysing them. I consider the idea that it might be a boy thing not to do this, but then I think of Nima's willingness to talk deeply about things, and I decide it's probably just a Sam thing. I guess that, for Sam, whatever happened between us is not a big deal, but just normal boy–girl interaction and it hasn't had an effect on our friendship. That's probably what Sam does with all his female friends so the best thing for me to do is to try to stop getting hysterical and over-analytical and just enjoy the friendship.

Even so, I'm still dying to know what happened with Stella and I realise that Sam is not going to bring it up. He's probably already forgotten about it, like he's forgotten about kissing me, so I seize the moment and ask, 'Don't you want to draw Stella instead? Wouldn't she be a better model?'

'Stella?' Sam says, taking a sip of his coffee. 'No actually, I don't want to draw Stella.'

'Why not? She's really pretty.'

'It's not all about being pretty,' Sam says, with a serious

expression now, fixing me with his blue gaze. 'Stella's a laugh, but that's all. I like you, Julia, because we like the same things. You're really interested in art, and I like talking to you. I also happen to think *you're* very pretty.'

Wow! I can't believe what Sam just said to me. He thinks I'm pretty! And he likes talking to me! Me! Who last year wasn't able to talk to anyone! Still, I must try not to let it go to my head – even though, coming from Sam, this is major revelation!

'So, do you want to do it?' he asks, seeing me look a bit thoughtful.

'Maybe . . . when? Where? Do we do it at the art class?'

'I don't think they'd let us do it there, but you can come to my house if you want or I can come to yours.'

'Your house,' I say quickly. The thought of Sam coming to my house for even a glass of water makes me break out in a sweat.

'Cool,' he says. 'What're you doing tomorrow?'

CHAPTER TWENTY-THREE

Brothers – Who Needs Them?

'I'm going to kill you, and that little fur ball!' Tony shouts, chasing me around the apartment. 'I told you from the beginning to keep that animal away from me!'

My brother has gone completely ballistic because Zoë has taken to using his sock drawer as a toilet. I suppose his hysteria is a bit understandable, since he's getting ready to go out with his Swedish girlfriend and he'd rather smell of Calvin Klein than cat poo when he meets her.

'It's not her fault!' I shout back as I jump over the sofa to get away from him. 'Try keeping your stupid drawer shut for once, she's only a kitten. She can't tell the difference between your sock drawer and the litter tray.' I'm all out of breath, partly from running and partly from laughing, which makes him even madder at me.

'It might only be a kitten, but if you don't do something about that animal soon, it's going to be an ex-kitten.'

'Calm down, Tony *mou*,' my mum says in her pacifying

129

tone as she walks past us towards his room with a can of air freshener.

Even though it's hilariously funny, secretly I must admit I would hate it if Zoë pooed in any of my drawers. I've been having real trouble getting her to go in her litter tray and no matter what I do, she would rather go in Tony's sock drawer instead. As an alternative solution to his problem, I suggested that he remove his socks from that drawer and just let her use it as a toilet, but that didn't go down very well at all.

Personally, I think she's doing it on purpose, because she knows that Tony hates her. It's a very well-known fact that cats are intelligent creatures and have an instinct about these things.

Of course, I've never had to do any litter training for a cat before. In Cyprus our entire backyard was a litter tray and Chloe just went out there and no one had to know anything about it. That's the downside to having a kitten, even an adorable one, in a second-floor flat in London.

Tony borrows some socks from Dad, then runs, shouting death threats at me, out of the flat to meet his hot date. My brother has had a succession of gorgeous blonde Scandinavian girlfriends. Perhaps, I think, and start giggling to myself, serial dating runs in the family.

I've been hiding in my bedroom since early this morning, and apart from shaving my gorilla legs and armpits, and bleaching my upper lip (as I refer to my moustache these days), I have also tried on every single piece of clothing that I own. I just don't know what to wear for this modelling thing this afternoon and I'm in a panic about it. Thankfully, Anna was free to come over for a chat and give me advice.

'Is he going to paint your portrait?' Anna asks, as I try on the tenth combination of clothes.

'Not sure . . .' I reply hesitantly. 'He said he wants to draw a person from real life. That's why it's called life drawing, I suppose.' I look in the mirror. 'What if he doesn't like it? Oh dear, I should have asked him what he wanted me to wear.'

'If he wanted you to look a specific way he would have asked you to dress accordingly,' Anna says, being very sensible as always. 'He obviously doesn't mind.'

'Oh, Anna,' I whinge, 'I just want to look really nice.'

'You *do* look really nice – and anyway, it's just a portrait. That's just your face isn't it? Besides,' Anna carries on, giving a little dig with her elbow, 'are you sure you want to look so nice? You might tempt him to start all that kissing stuff again and remember what you promised yourself? To be a good girl?'

'You're right. I'm just panicking,' I say and we agree that I should be casual, in jeans, cowboy boots and a lacy vintage blouse I bought in Camden Market.

'This way if he decides to do the portrait as a head and shoulders, he can include a bit of the lace in to give it texture,' I explain.

'Mmm . . . yes . . . texture, that sounds good,' she says, and I know she is teasing me, like she always does when I say anything remotely arty. 'Does your mum know you're going to his house?'

'Are you joking?' I say with a hollow laugh. 'My mum doesn't even know he exists . . . well, I suppose she knows he exists as he phones me a lot, but all she knows is that he's a boy from my art class.'

'So, let me guess: officially, we are going out together this afternoon, then?' Anna says, giving me a raised eyebrow.

'Well, I could say that we're spending the rest of the day together, I guess . . . ?'

'Fine, so long I know what I'm supposed to be doing and what to tell my mum in case she sees yours.'

Thank God for best girl friends I think, and give Anna a hug.

CHAPTER TWENTY-FOUR

Art Lesson

My hands are trembling slightly and my heart is thumping as I press Sam's doorbell. Standing outside his double-fronted terraced house in Muswell Hill, I check again, for at least the tenth time, the piece of paper in my hand with his address on it. It took me forever to find the house, and since it's not near the Tube station, I had to secretly borrow my brother's A–Z to look up the street. This is the first time I've made my own way to anyone's house. Since I've been in England, when I've visited a house for the first time, either my dad's taken me there or I've gone with a friend. While I'm obviously feeling very nervous, I'm also feeling quite proud of myself for managing to arrive in one piece *and* on time.

As Sam closes the door behind me, he says, 'Just go all the way up the stairs till you can't go any further. My room is right at the top.'

The house is huge and the staircase seems to go on for ever. While we climb the stairs through three different floors, I get glimpses into some of the other rooms. I see a bedroom painted in shades of red and purple with a huge double bed under a bay window draped with lavish curtains, then a small boy's bedroom full of toys and books, and a luxurious bathroom in white and grey marble.

'I use my bedroom as a work space too,' Sam explains as we make our way up. 'I do everything up there. In fact, it's where I spend most of my time. It's great having the loft room.' Finally, the stairs stop outside a blue spray-painted door and, after pushing it open, he stands back politely for me to go in. Sam's bedroom really does seem to be in the roof, as it has a sloping ceiling and wooden beams, which are all covered in posters.

There are also posters and pictures all over the walls, the wardrobe and the door. The only place that's not covered in pictures is the huge window through which the afternoon sun streams in to form a pool of light in the middle of the floor like a spotlight.

'I'll go and get us a drink,' Sam says, and puts on some music. 'Have a seat.' He points to an orange beanbag chair next to a pile of papers and some paintbrushes on the floor. 'I won't be a minute.'

The sound of reggae fills the room and I drop my bag on to the carpet and flop into the beanbag while he runs downstairs to get us some tea.

Sam's room is twice the size of mine, but is jam-packed with all sorts of things. Magazines, records, paper, pencils, books, tubes of paint and paintbrushes all over the place. My room, even if my mum complains about it, is tidy in comparison to this. Since it's small, I *have* to keep things in their place.

I look around, taking everything in. Sam's bed, a futon almost on the floor, has a blue and white striped duvet cover crumpled up in a heap in the middle of it, and there's a TV at the foot of the bed. In one corner of the room I see a record player with a pile of vinyls next to it and, in another, an overflowing laundry basket. There's also a wardrobe, a desk covered in all sorts of things, and loads of shelves bursting with books and board games.

I decide that I really like Sam's room. It's cosy, even if it's a mess. Feeling less anxious now, I relax back into the beanbag chair and wait for him to come back with our tea. While I'm scanning the images stuck on the walls, I notice the poster from the surrealist exhibition we saw together at the Tate, and smile at the memory of that day. I get a bit of a jolt though, when I realise that now both Sam and Nima have the same poster stuck on their bedroom wall. Sinking further into the chair, I give myself up to the sound of Bob Marley, watching the myriad dust particles dance to the beat of the music in the beam of light from the window. As if entranced, I wonder if Sam will kiss me again today.

Here I go again. Brain on overdrive, fantasising about Sam and getting myself all hormonal and wound up again. So, I wonder, are chemistry and hormones the only things that motivate us, and is our brain mainly guided by our sexual urges? If human beings are slaves to these urges, are we really as civilised as we think we are? Isn't self-control one of the qualities that is supposed to mark the difference between us and the rest of the animal kingdom? How can I make all these promises about resisting and keep my butterfly wings to myself, yet sit here in Sam's bedroom wistfully longing for him to take me in his arms and snog me senseless?

The door opens suddenly, making me jump out of my skin. Sam enters, carrying two steaming mugs of tea and a biscuit tin under his arm. Sam is always carrying too many things, I think, remembering when I first met him, and then I smile at him.

'Here you go,' he says, handing me one of the mugs, then sits down on the floor beside me and helps himself to a biscuit. 'Everybody's out,' he says, with his mouth full, 'so we can work without being interrupted – not that anyone comes up here anyway. My little brother doesn't dare. He knows it would be more than his life's worth.' He laughs.

'How old is your brother?' I ask him, trying to imagine a miniature version of Sam.

'Eleven – going on *five*, the way my mum treats him,' he says, rolling his eyes. 'He's a real pest.'

Oh no, I think – that's probably what *my* brother says about me! And the thought of my brother, which I try instantly to dismiss, causes me to start hyperventilating. I can only imagine what he would say if he knew his little sister was alone with a boy in his bedroom, in an empty house, on a Sunday afternoon.

'Do you fancy a smoke?' Sam asks, while he's changing the music. 'Oh, I forgot. You don't smoke, do you?' he adds, before I can reply. Then he walks towards me and pulls me off the beanbag chair and into his arms with one strong pull. Before I even register what's happening, we've got our arms wrapped around each other and we're kissing for Britain – well, maybe him for Britain and me for Cyprus. My knees practically give way underneath me and I'm glad Sam's got his arms around my waist, or I think I might fall in a heap on the floor.

After what seems like days we come up for air and Sam says, 'Shall we start the drawing while it's still light?'

Oh, right, the drawing . . . I completely forgot why I was there. 'Fine . . . yes . . .' I mumble, smoothing my hair down and trying to regain my composure.

'I think you can sit back on the beanbag actually,' he says and starts arranging his drawing board in front of the chair. 'It's a nice shape and you can just relax into it.'

Sitting back on the beanbag I try to relax, but feel awkward. 'What do you want me to do?' I ask.

'Oh, just take your clothes off and get comfortable,' Sam says, with his back to me as he rummages through his art materials for the right number pencil.

CHAPTER TWENTY-FIVE

Laughing It Off

'Don't lie!' Linda exclaims excitedly in a high-pitched voice, her eyes bulging. It's Monday morning during break, and obviously I've just told her about Sam, and this time I told her about the kissing and everything. I just had to, or else I was going to explode. 'You *are* joking aren't you?' she asks, a bit calmer now, and she leans in closer to look me in the eyes. The kissing bit didn't bother Linda at all. 'Oh, it doesn't surprise me one bit,' she said, when I told her. 'I saw it coming ages ago,' but the getting naked thing blew her away. 'Did he actually mean, like, take your clothes off, as in strip totally naked, or just take your jumper and shoes off naked?' she carried on squeaking.

Linda doesn't give me a chance to answer.

'What a bloody cheek!' she then explodes. 'What the hell did you say to him?'

'Well, apparently life drawing means drawing someone naked, and since I'm an art student I should have known all about it and not have been so shocked and mortally offended.'

'Well, Miss Ignoramus,' Linda says, bursting out laughing at me now. 'You tricked that poor boy into thinking you know more about art than you do! I wouldn't have had a clue what life drawing meant either, but then I have an excuse, because I know nothing about art.'

'I bet Scarlet knows what it means. She's a real artist, or at least her mum is. She wouldn't have got herself in this mess,' I say, feeling my face go red at the memory.

'So, what did you say to him?'

'I sort of went numb and deaf and sort of said "Pardon?" like an idiot. And he just said, "You know, take your clothes off for the life drawing?" And I just said pardon again . . . like a moron this time. Oh God, Linda, don't make me go through what I said to him again, because I think I will have to kill myself. It's so embarrassing. All I know is that I felt like a fool and got offended that he would imagine that I would just take all my clothes off just like that, so I just left.'

'And how did you leave it? Did you fall out? Are you going to see each other again?'

'I really don't know, I can't remember. Sam was just being Sam and said something like, "Cool, no worries," or something, and I left so quickly I'm not sure if we fell out. But I'll have to see him again on Saturday at the art class and I'm dreading it.'

'Were you really pissed off with him?'

'Mostly just embarrassed. I like him and all that, but I think it was a bit much to expect me to take my clothes off just like that for him, even for art's sake. In my country you just don't do that, even if you are good friends, unless you are going to have sex.'

'I think Sam's a bit of a chancer, actually,' Linda says with a giggle. 'It's a very good excuse to get a girl to take her clothes off. It's only art . . . honest! Yeah, right! So, do you think that's what he was hoping for? Do you think he thought you were going to have sex even though he knows you've got a boyfriend and everything?'

'I don't know . . . I suppose so . . . maybe . . . I just don't know with him. He's so laid back, maybe it was just a life drawing thing, but . . .'

'But you *do* fancy him,' Linda says, dropping her voice to almost a whisper now. 'Would you consider doing it with him?'

'Oh God, no! Snogging is one thing, but having sex is something else completely, I'm really not up for that yet – especially with someone who isn't even my boyfriend! I wouldn't have minded if we'd just carried on snogging a bit more though. Oh God, Linda, it's probably all my fault because he knows I like snogging him, but I definitely couldn't get naked and have sex . . . I'm not even at that stage with Nima. I'm not ready for sex with anyone just yet. Would *you* have?'

'What? Have sex with Sam?' she says, giggling now. 'Mmm . . . maybe, I don't know. He is pretty gorgeous, but no, seriously, I don't think I'm anywhere near ready for that either, and besides Ali's only just started to kiss me for longer than a split second.'

'Boys are nothing but trouble.'

'Yeah, but poor Nima's no trouble, is he?' Linda says, in his defence.

'No, it's true . . .' I say, and start thinking that Nima has never, in all the time I've known him, given me any trouble. On the other hand, though, he has never got me as excited or as wound up as I seem to feel with Sam either.

Suddenly I start considering the possibility that perhaps Nima and I might not have what it takes to get the sparks going, whatever that really is. Maybe there's no chemistry between us. Of course I really do like Nima. In fact, I kind of love Nima, but he just doesn't get me churned up and desperate to kiss him, even if I do love being with him, and think he is gorgeous.

'We are all so bloody complicated!' I sigh at Linda, who gives me a perplexed look. Just then we see Scarlet running towards us from across the playground, shouting and waving her arms about.

'Been looking for you two all morning,' she says, out of breath. 'What's up?'

So I explain.

'Ha ha ha . . . and more ha!' Scarlet says, holding her sides from laughing. 'He should come to my mum's life drawing classes, since he's so keen – she holds them every

Tuesday evening in her studio.' Then she starts laughing again. 'She has a couple of old wrinklies she uses as nude models – a man and a woman who take turns posing alternate weeks. I've even drawn them a few times. But I don't suppose they're exactly what Sam has in mind . . .' she adds and we fall about laughing.

CHAPTER TWENTY-SIX

Bribery Does the Trick

'Iouliaaaa! You won't believe what I've got for you . . .' my mum shouts excitedly, as she walks through the front door of our flat on Saturday afternoon. 'Quick, come and see!'

I've been sitting at my desk all morning, trying to do homework, in an effort to keep away from all boys, while little Zoë sleeps curled up on my lap. I faked bad period pains so that I could miss my art class. I can't face seeing Sam just yet, but trying to concentrate on school work has not been an easy task. All I've been able to think about is Sam and Nima, and going from feeling guilty and confused to feeling annoyed with myself for not keeping my promises to myself, and feeling bad about Nima, and offended with Sam that he would imagine I'd strip naked for him just like that. In fact, I keep wishing I was in Cyprus where I don't remember having these problems with boys. I can't wait to go back there for the whole summer.

I know I should be happy with the way things are going

here, especially since I took the plunge and told Nima everything about Sam. Well, not exactly everything. I definitely didn't mention anything about the life drawing incident, or any details about the snogging. I just told him that although Sam and I started out just as good friends it sort of got to be a bit more than just friendship, which I suppose could imply that maybe we did kiss, but that I would put a stop to it, and promised Nima I wouldn't go out with Sam again. The trouble is, I'm not sure whether I feel better or worse for telling him. Linda and Anna think it was the right thing to do. And I'm not even sure how Nima feels about it either. When I did finally tell him about Sam, his reaction was so calm and civilised it was hard to tell if he was upset or not, which confused me even more, since he's usually so ready to talk about things. Luckily Nima is definitely not a person given to hysterics.

'It's your life,' Nima said to me when I told him, 'but I'm glad that you've made a choice.' When I told the girls about his reaction they were amazed that he was so understanding. 'Maybe he doesn't mind,' I told them, half jokingly but half serious. 'Maybe Nima's had enough and doesn't care if we stay together or not . . . let's face it – I've been a bit of a pain lately.'

The truth is, I don't want to split up with Nima. I like him too much and we've been together for ages – and besides I want to see if this chemistry thing can exist between us.

The whole Sam saga has really shaken me up and has

highlighted yet again how much more there is for me to learn about life in England. I know it's not only about cultural differences but culture does have something to do with it. I'm sure an English girl would have handled all that stuff with Sam a bit better than I would. Linda thinks it's just teenage hormones but I think it's also not quite understanding how things work here. Perhaps going back to Cyprus as soon as possible for a fix of my old life and friends is what I need to straighten me out.

'Come, Ioulia *mou*, come and see . . .' my mum shouts again from the living room. So I remove Zoë from my lap and get up to see what all the fuss is about, but nearly fall flat on my face. Both of my legs have gone dead from keeping them so still as Zoë has been asleep on my lap for hours and I didn't have the heart to push her off.

'Look what *Kyria* Maria has sent you!' my mum says, when I finally make it to the living room. She delves into one of the four carrier bags she has come home with, pulling out a pair of black and brown striped trousers.

'Why?' I ask. 'Where from?' The trousers are actually really cool. 'Why has she sent me clothes?'

'I thought I told you that Ari's parents have a factory that makes clothes, didn't I?'

'No, I had no idea, I thought they had a Greek restaurant,' I say and start rummaging through the bags. Incredibly, I discover that Ari's mum is making the trendiest clothes in London and most of them for Miss Selfridge! I can't believe my luck! I'm in a complete state of euphoria.

'What? She gave you all this stuff for me as a present? Why?'

'Because she likes you,' my mum says grinning. 'She just said to pick whatever I wanted for you and to bring you down to the factory some time so you can pick what you want for yourself. Do you like what I've chosen?'

I'm in heaven! There are two pairs of fantastic trousers, loads of tops, a brilliant denim miniskirt, a red jumper with buttons all down the back, and a corduroy jacket! I'm completely bowled over that a) my mum has such good taste, and b) that she'd made a friend who is nearly as useful as *Kyria* Eva and her mystic coffee cup. In fact I might go as far as to say that Ari's mum is almost ahead in the usefulness department to even *Kyria* Eva and her fortune-telling skills.

'I love it all, Mama,' I say. I don't know what to try on first.

'You should call and say thank you,' my mum suggests and starts dialling their number, handing me the receiver before I have a chance to agree. Instead of *Kyria* Maria though, I hear Ari's voice answer the phone.

'Oh! Oh . . . hi Ari,' I say all flustered. 'Can I speak to your mum?'

'Hello, Julia,' he replies, recognising my voice. 'What's wrong with speaking to me?'

Here we go again. I can't believe it – I'm trying to avoid talking to anyone from the opposite sex and my mum lands me in it again.

'No . . . nothing . . . Hello, Ari,' I say, and before he passes the phone to his mum, we've made a date to meet up that evening.

'Your dad will drop you off at their house,' my mum says, visibly pleased about the arrangement, when I get off the phone.

'No Mum, please. He's coming to pick me up from here,' I say, *dis*pleased with myself for being so impossibly weak and feeble and breaking my promise about keeping away from boys who aren't Nima for a bit! Honestly, I'm hopeless and not to be trusted with keeping any promises.

CHAPTER TWENTY-SEVEN

Changing Times

'I obviously have a problem with saying no,' I say to Anna the next day. We're sitting on her bedroom floor, talking. Anna's room is a real sanctuary for both of us. Apart from the fact that it's cosy and warm, it's also the room where our friendship began, when our families were sharing a house. It feels good to sit there listening to Greek music, eating Greek sweets and drinking Greek coffee with the door shut to the rest of the world.

'I don't think it's just you,' Anna says sympathetically. 'We all have that problem sometimes.'

'I don't think you are as bad as me,' I reply thoughtfully. 'You know Anna, Ari's really sweet,' I say, in an attempt to explain to her and myself why I'm bothering to introduce yet another boy into my already complicated life. 'He took me out for a meal and we talked for hours. He's very mature for his age. Being Greek is not easy even for a boy it seems. He's got loads of problems with his parents about what they want him to study and what girls to go out with . . . His parents are worse than ours.'

'How? What do you mean?' Anna asks in amazement.

'Oh God, I don't know, like, he wants to be a musician. And his parents want him to be a lawyer. If he goes out with an English girl they don't like it. Can you believe that? They are so old-fashioned. It's like they were born in the nineteenth century. He was born here, for Christ's sake! They don't see how things have changed since they left Cyprus. Anyway, I like him. I think we'll be good friends . . . and he's really good-looking. Not that I need to get into that with him. I've got enough on my plate as it is,' I say laughing.

'Yes, I agree,' Anna replies, laughing too.

'It's down to that butterfly syndrome thing my mum was talking about,' I say, and we giggle. 'I blame those wings . . . but yours don't seem to get you into as much trouble as mine. How come?'

'Oh, I'm just boring, or maybe I just don't know how to use them properly,' she says, laughing. 'But I'm looking forward to spreading my wings as wide as possible and tasting the pollen too. I need to make up for lost time when I go to university.'

The way time is passing by, Anna will have gone off to university before I know it and the thought makes me a bit uneasy. God knows how different things will be then and she won't be around to talk to. So much has changed in such a short time for both of us since coming to

England. For me, every month that passes seems to make a major difference to my life – whether it's my English, finding my way around London, making new friends, or trying to sort how I feel about the boys in my life.

'I will miss you so much, Anna,' I say, feeling suddenly gloomy at the thought of losing her. 'You are my soulmate. What will I do without you? I can't bear to be separated from you as well as Sophia.'

'Don't be silly, you'll come and visit and stay with me – it will be so great, away from home and everything. Students are famous for parties, you know. The first year especially is meant to be one big party. It'll be great, you'll see.'

We both cheer up considerably at the thought of escaping parental and brotherly surveillance.

CHAPTER TWENTY-EIGHT

Roll On, Summer

The spring term is really galloping along now and there is a freshness in the air which I can feel on the way to school in the mornings. The winter gloom seems to be slowly giving way to longer, brighter days as we approach the end of March, and the thought of the Easter holidays lifts my spirits and reminds me that summer and my trip to Cyprus will soon follow.

Ever since I promised Nima I wouldn't go out with Sam again I've been really good and these days I only see Sam at art class on Saturdays. I was absolutely dreading seeing him for the first time, after our life drawing fiasco, but eventually I had to face him. Typical of Sam, though, he made it really easy. He acted as if nothing had ever happened. No mention of getting naked or life drawings, or anything embarrassing, and I was certainly not going to bring it up. I have tried to erase it from my memory, even though it often comes back to haunt me. Everything seems to have gone back to normal with Sam, apart from my finding excuses not to go anywhere with him after the class. Since I had never officially gone out with him in the first place, there was not much I could say or explain apart from making out I was busy. I mean, I couldn't exactly break it off with him since there was nothing to break off. So, as much as I found it really difficult and still felt attracted to Sam, I just kept my lips to myself and avoided any situation with him that could lead to snogging.

I was glad I managed to keep my promise to Nima and, as Anna said, just 'concentrate' on him and not have to juggle everything and everyone else around me. Although I never *actually* lied to Nima, I still felt guilty about my behaviour. Anyway, I decided that cooling down my social life a bit was the best thing to do.

I must admit that even though Nima's reaction was calm and collected when I first told him how I felt about Sam, I have sensed a change in him. Frankly, I don't blame him. Nima is not stupid and he probably feels that even though I've kept my promise, my heart's not completely in it, if the conversation I had with him a few days ago is anything to go by.

'Do you still see Sam at your art class on Saturdays?' Nima had asked, giving me a long hard look as we sat on the bus after school.

'Yes, I do,' I say casually. 'Why do you ask?'

'Just wondering,' he said, and looked away.

'I see him at the class and that's all,' I continued, and

since it's the truth, I didn't break out into my usual red blotches.

'Don't you go out for a coffee sometimes? I thought you said you were good mates.'

'We *are* friends, and that's all we are,' I tried to explain. 'I promised that I wouldn't go out with him, and I'm keeping my promise. Besides, Nima, as you know I'm not going out as much these days.'

I decided that spending a bit more time on my school work, and my friends, and less time obsessing about boys was not such a bad idea, especially after what's happened since that time I went out with Ari.

Ari's mum thinks she's found a daughter-in-law. Really! What's she thinking of? I went out with Ari a couple of times to the cinema and for a meal, because he's nice and we are good friends. Now the whole family thinks I'm his future bride. I'm fifteen years old for goodness' sake, does she seriously think I'm going to be thinking about a long-term relationship with anyone at my age? I mean, I love all the clothes that she gives me and everything, but once I realised that she was doing it because she thought I was a member of the family, it's definitely put a negative slant on accepting the gifts. What's worse, I get the feeling that *Kyria* Maria is so relieved that her son finally likes a Greek girl that she is going to hang on to me come what may. My mum also seems to think it's a good idea that I see Ari and she keeps encouraging me to go out with him and his crowd. I complain to her that his mum is being a bit presumptuous.

'They're a good family and he seems a nice boy,' she keeps saying.

'Mum, we don't have arranged marriages in Cyprus any more, remember? Even *you* didn't have one and we're in England now, so stop pushing me to get involved.'

'I'm not suggesting you get married,' she says, horrified. 'Just keep up the contact.'

'*You* might not be suggesting anything of the sort, but try telling Ari's mother and grandmother that.'

In fact Ari's grandmother now thinks I'm engaged to her grandson and makes even more of a fuss of me when I visit. As much as I like her, this is all too worrying. In a village like the one she comes from, if a girl is seen in public with a boy more than once then she is most definitely engaged to be married or else she is a loose woman and not suitable to be part of a respectable family.

Ari, my mum tells me in a confidential voice, is quite close to a Jewish girl that he's been seeing for ages and *Kyria* Maria is more than a bit concerned she might end up with a Jewish daughter-in-law. What my mother doesn't know is that Ari has already mentioned this girl to me and the fact that his mother is desperate to get him away from her. He was really sweet and open and told me all about it. I felt so comfortable with him that I told him about Nima and Sam and everything, which was brilliant.

It is so great to have a Greek boy as a friend and be able to talk about all this stuff. He really seems to understand me, although I did notice him glaze over a bit when I started obsessing over Sam and Nima. But he's a boy, so I suppose my talking too much about my emotional angst does his head in. So once again, thank God for my girl friends!

Ari's parents are very religious and they want their children to marry into the Greek Orthodox faith. Honestly! The things grown-ups think about. I can't believe it. He's only seventeen and he's only going out with this girl, so where marriage comes into it I have no idea. Mind you, Greeks are very big on weddings and, in Cyprus, especially in the villages, it is a massive affair. They go on for three days and three nights. Thousands of people are invited (their entire village and the neighbouring ones), and there is enough food and drink to feed everyone twice over. The celebrations start the day before the wedding and then, after the church ceremony, they have a huge feast with music, dancing, eating and drinking for the next few days. Weddings usually take place in the summer in Cyprus, so tables are laid out in the open air and very often, because there are so many tables, they are put either in the village square or in a field somewhere. Everyone has to traipse around in their wedding-day best, new shoes and all, in the newly ploughed earth but no one cares because it's such brilliant fun. The Greek Cypriots in England do a similar thing, only in some big, posh hotel with slightly fewer guests and not lasting quite so long, but the principle remains the same. Everyone has fun! The best bit is when the bride and groom get up to dance and everyone pins paper money on their clothes as a wedding gift. By the end of the dance every bit of them is covered in money and only their faces are visible. So, I suppose Ari's mum is anxious because she wants to have this style of 'Big Fat Greek Wedding' for all her kids.

Here I am though, having decided to become a semi-recluse, verging on becoming a nun, staying at home with my cat. Well, apart from sometimes seeing Nima, that is – and the girls, and Ari, and Sam at my Saturday class.

Oh God, roll on summer, is all I can say. I need to get away from everyone and sort myself out. I long to see my cousins and my grandfather and the rest of my family. No complicated relationships there. I can't escape the thought that if I were in Cyprus, my life would be so much simpler.

CHAPTER TWENTY-NINE

A Call From Home

In fact, things get worse.

I watch my mother's face turn ashen and see her hand start to tremble as she holds the receiver to her ear. I stand by the kitchen door feeling sick to my stomach with the anticipation of something bad as I try to make out what's wrong. I gather from the conversation that she is talking to my auntie Eleni in Cyprus. This is a worrying fact in itself since my auntie hates the telephone and would do anything rather than use it, so it must be bad news.

'How is he now?' my mum is saying in a choked-up voice. 'Will he stay in hospital long?' Oh my God, I think. It must be my *bapu*. Who else could they be talking about? I stand right up close to the phone, trying to hear what my auntie is saying.

'Fine, yes, I understand,' my mum finally says and puts the phone down slowly.

'What, Mama? What happened?' I ask her, on the verge of tears. 'Is everything OK? Is it *Bapu*?'

'Yes,' she says, in a weak voice, 'he's had a fall, he's in the hospital,' and her eyes well up with tears.

'How? Where?' I ask, panicking.

'He was on a ladder picking lemons from the trees in the orchard, when he lost his balance and fell off,' she explains. 'They think he's all right, but he's got concussion, and because of his age they are concerned.'

My grandfather is never ill – or has ever given anybody any cause for concern. He's such a robust person. My mum is two thousand miles away from her dad and I see the worry etched on her face.

'Oh Mama, I'm sure he'll be all right, *Bapu* is so strong,' I tell her and put my arms around her, though I'm still shaking.

'I wish I was there . . . I should be there . . .' she says, wiping away her tears.

'I think you must definitely go and see him,' my dad tells my mum after dinner while we're discussing *bapu*'s accident, 'and you should take Ioulia with you too. Her school is breaking up for the Easter holidays next week and he'll want to see both of you.'

I can't believe what I'm hearing! If I wasn't so worried about my *bapu* I would be jumping with joy. My dad can be so wonderful sometimes. Easter apparently comes very early this year in England while the Greek one is not till May because they use a different calendar for religious events in Cyprus. So we would be back in London again in good time to celebrate our Greek Easter with my dad and Tony.

'Anyway,' he carries on, 'I think she deserves it since she didn't go at Christmas and she's been such a good girl.' Right now my dad is definitely scoring some major I-have-the-best-dad-the-world points with me.

'You're right, Dad,' my brother says, interrupting the conversation, after an unusually long spell of silence following the news of *Bapu*'s fall. 'You must both go and see him. We'll be fine here – you mustn't worry. Dad and I will take care of things.' I stare at him in total amazement at this unusually mature and grown-up attitude. 'I'll even feed your cat,' he adds, with a brotherly smile, leaving me completely gobsmacked. I decide that he must have had a bump on the head too, as he's being so nice to me for a change. I'm really touched by Tony's reaction and realise how worried he must be too about our *bapu*. I got so used to him being grumpy and moody all the time that I forgot how much I really love my brother.

'Oh, thank you, Tony,' my mum says, her voice sounding shaky.

'Are you sure you don't mind looking after Zoë?' I ask, feeling very grateful. 'I can always take her to Anna's.'

'Don't worry about it. Besides, I plan to instil some discipline into that fur ball while you're out of the way,' he says with a laugh.

Suddenly I'm filled with love and pride for my dear

older brother and I walk over to where he's sitting and give him a big hug.

Even though I'm worried about my *bapu*, I'm also really excited to be going to Cyprus and I can't wait to get to school and tell Linda. I know she'll be pleased for me, which is more than I can say for Nima, who didn't seem very understanding when I told him on the bus this morning.

'Why do *you* need to go?' he asked me, which I thought was a bit insensitive. 'It's the Easter holidays and we could have spent some time together.'

'Because my *bapu* is ill and I'm worried about him, and my mum wants me to go with her,' I replied, thinking that this did not sound like the usual thoughtful and caring Nima.

'You don't look very worried. In fact, you can't stop grinning . . . You look like you can't wait to get away,' he said, getting himself into an even bigger huff.

That isn't fair. I *hadn't* been grinning that much, and he knows how much I love my *bapu*. 'That's not true, I told him I just want to go back to my country and see my family and my *bapu* . . . I can't believe you're making such a big deal out of this, Nima . . .'

'Oh, just go then!' he said, and his eyes were full of sparks. 'But I'm not sure I'll be here when you get back . . .'

'Oh Nima, you are being really difficult and unreasonable,' I said, thinking that his outburst really didn't make sense. Was he breaking up with me because of this, after everything else that went on?

'I don't know, maybe it's for the best. We could probably do with a break from each other,' he said finally, and got off the bus.

I watched him walk away and tried to collect my feelings. I couldn't tell whether I was heartbroken, wanted to cry or wanted to throw a heavy object at him. I couldn't believe he was giving me such a hard time over this. Nice, lovely, thoughtful Nima finally snapped at me over something that can't be helped. What does it mean? Are we finished?

Part of me doesn't believe it could be over. I think Nima is just throwing a wobbly and will calm down when he has time to think about it. I would have expected him to throw a strop like when I told him about Sam, and I would have deserved it then, but not this! I think he's being unreasonable, but I will still call him tonight and see if we can talk it through on the phone.

It's probably not a bad idea to have a break from him and everyone else for a bit though. This trip to Cyprus has come at an ideal time.

'How long will you be going for?' Linda whispers to me a little later, during yet another excruciatingly mind-numbing geography lesson which I nearly missed on account of being late for school after the episode with Nima.

'For the whole of the Easter holidays,' I whisper back, as I point to Cyprus on the world map spread out in front of us on the desk.

'Lucky cow,' she whispers behind her hand, then points at the south of Spain. 'That's where I'd like to be if I can't go with you . . .'

Now that's a thought I like – Linda coming with me. But I quickly remember that this is not the right time, since the main reason for our visit is to be with my grandfather.

'Have you told Nima and Sophia yet?' Linda asks me, once we are finally set free.

'Yes, and yes. Sophia was over the moon and Nima was a bit under it,' I say with a slight smile, but then the memory of Nima flouncing off the bus brings me down again.

'Oh, very clever,' Linda says and gives me a little shove. 'Making jokes in English now, are we? So what did he say?'

'I think we've decided to break it off for a bit,' I say, and I'm surprised that I feel a lump rising in my throat.

'What? What does that mean, for a bit?' Linda squeaks.

'Well, we thought we would have a break from each other and see how we feel after the holidays. I think . . .'

'Who's idea was that?' she asks, looking at me with big eyes.

'Sort of Nima's . . .' I reply and I can't quite believe what I'm saying. 'We had this big row, he flipped out and got all unreasonable, saying, "OK then, go! But don't

162

expect me to be here when you come back," or something like that – all dramatic and so unlike him!'

'No! I don't believe you! What made him say that?'

'Nothing! I just said that I was going to Cyprus for Easter because my *bapu* is ill . . . but I think he didn't like the way I told him with a great big grin on my face . . .'

'Well, are you upset? Do you want to break up with Nima?'

'I'm very upset. Honestly, Linda, I don't want to finish with Nima – especially over this! After all that agonising and trying to keep it all together and everything. I wouldn't have gone through all that if I didn't like him . . . if he didn't mean anything . . . This is really stupid.'

'Did you say that to him?'

'I didn't really get a chance. He just flounced off the bus, and I just sat there in a state of shock.'

Linda, seeing how upset I am, puts an arm around my shoulder. 'What are you going to do?' she asks in a soft voice.

'I'll call him when I get home and try to talk it through with him,' I reply, swallowing hard. 'I can't believe he really means it . . . well, at least I hope he doesn't. It's true that I looked happy when I told him, because I *am* happy to be going to Cyprus, but he said I looked like I couldn't wait to get away. To be honest, it's true, I can't wait to go – but it's not because I can't wait to get away from him. It's *everything*.'

'Well, that's nice! You want to get away from all your

friends?' Linda says with a smile, trying to make light of the conversation and cheer me up. 'Thank you very much, Miss Loyalty.'

'Not from you! I don't want to get away from *you*, Linda. I just want to have a break from everything here. I want to get away from all the complications with boys and get my feelings into perspective. I feel as if I don't know which way to turn at the moment or what I want. I just want to see the sun and my family and old friends again, and make sure my grandfather is OK . . . that's all.'

CHAPTER THIRTY

Home Again

Tears are running down my cheeks uncontrollably, blurring my vision and making it difficult to negotiate the steps off the plane. But contrary to how it might appear, it's not sorrow. I'm laughing, and shedding tears of pure happiness to be on Cyprus soil again.

The warm spring breeze is caressing my hair and the sea looks bluer and sparklier than I've ever seen it. Larnaka airport might be just another run-of-the-mill boring place for most people who land there, but for me it's the most beautiful airport in the world. It's so close to the water you feel like you are on a thrilling roller-coaster ride as you land, and that the plane is going to dip its wings in the sea. Once you've landed, the ride continues by speeding along the runway which is parallel to the beach, so the first thing to greet you is the deep blue of the Mediterranean.

'I can't believe we are here,' my mum says to me. We're both feeling dazed and emotional. I want to put my arms around her and give her a hug, but we are both carrying so many bags it feels like we're bringing half of Oxford Street with us. There are gifts for everyone. My mum also went to visit *Kyria* Maria's factory and bought a load of clothes at a discount for all my cousins. I can't wait to go through it all with Sophia – who will have first pick.

Sophia took the day off from school to come and collect us and I can hardly contain my excitement. For the first time since the dreaded phone call, that sinking feeling of worry about my *bapu* leaves me and it's replaced with pure joy at the prospect of seeing everyone again.

As the sliding doors to the arrivals lounge open, I get a glimpse of Sophia's head straining impatiently to see who is coming through. Finally, struggling with our huge trolley, my mum and I push our way out into the huge crowd of people who have come to meet their family and friends. I see Sophia and my uncle standing and waiting behind some barriers with loads of other people. She looks fabulous as always – her hair a little shorter than last summer and she is wearing a coat and a chunky woolly scarf in shades of purple and pink. It's strange seeing her in winter clothes. The last time we met it was summer in London and we walked about in summer clothes, and the last time I was in Cyprus it was August and boiling hot, so for some reason I thought I'd see everyone dressed for warm weather.

I stand rooted to the spot for a moment looking at her, then I'm suddenly overcome by a desperate urge to run to her, but the stupid barrier is in the way. I can see Sophia bouncing up and down in an agitated way, hands clasped in front of her chest, and then, unable to contain herself any more, she jumps over the barrier and runs to me, screaming with joy. As we stand in the middle of the walkway blocking everyone's path, we hug and kiss and scream with happiness. No one seems to mind. They all walk round us laughing, while my uncle, leading my mum and the trolley to one side, starts calling for us to follow him.

Sitting in my uncle's car with Sophia, I feel delirious with happiness to be back home in Cyprus again. We can't stop hugging and kissing each other and squealing like a couple of four-year-olds. As the car speeds along the familiar road to Nicosia, my eyes can't take in enough of what I see through the window. The last time I was on this road it was that fateful August day we left Cyprus for England, over a year and a half ago. The heat was unbearable then and the sun had scorched everything in sight, making the landscape look dry and barren, but it's a completely different picture now. Thanks to the winter rain, spring in Cyprus is the most beautiful season. My eyes feast on the green and lush landscape. The roadside is laced with yellow mimosa trees in bloom and the fields are covered in yellow daisies and red poppies. There are orchards full of lemon and orange trees, laden with fruit. I want to run out and throw myself in a field, roll around, and pick wild anemones with Sophia, like we did when we were little.

'Oh my God, Ioulia *mou*, this is the best thing that's happened to me so far this year,' Sophia says, holding my hand really tightly. 'Especially now we've been told by *Bapu*'s doctor that he's going to be fine.'

I hear my mum and my uncle discussing their father, our *bapu*, in the front of the car. 'It was touch and go,' my uncle is saying to my mum. 'For a minute there we thought we'd lost him.' His words alarm me. Even though I know he's fine, I won't feel sure until I see him.

'Oh my goodness! Who is this young lady?' Auntie Eleni says to me, as she reaches to embrace me. My auntie seems to have shrunk – I don't remember ever bending down to kiss her before, but then I realise that it's probably me who's got taller. Wiping away tears with a white lace handkerchief, my beloved auntie steps back to look at me.

'I'm not sure I would recognise her if I saw her in the street,' she tells my mother, smiling, and starts spitting at me – well, not actually spitting, but making a spitting sound which is a sort of special custom meant to keep the evil eye and bad spirits at bay. People with the evil eye can cause harm to the person they dislike through their insincere praises. To stop this happening, every time you're praised, someone has to spit at you, because you never know who has the evil eye. So beware – if you ever get praised by a Greek, expect to be spat at too!

My auntie is not the only one who thinks I've changed. All my relatives look shocked and amazed when they see me, because according to them, they barely recognise me. This doesn't thrill me a great deal. I mean, honestly, how much can a person change in just over a year and a half? And who wants to hear that their own flesh and blood doesn't recognise them? The only one who knows immediately who I am is my *bapu*.

'Hello, Ioulia *mou*, I knew you'd come back soon,' *Bapu* says to me the minute he sees me and I burst into tears as soon as I hug him. I sit next to him on the sofa in his house and realise with shock how much thinner and weaker he looks since I last saw him.

'Now don't let this frail body fool you,' he says with a chuckle when he sees that I'm upset. 'I'm as tough as Costa's donkey and I'll be back on that old ladder again picking lemons before you know it,' then he leans over and whispers in my ear, 'but only if you promise to hold it for me this time.'

I laugh. While I'm talking to my grandfather, I suddenly see Chloe walk through the open door and watch her slowly making her way over to me from across the room. Gingerly at first, she circles round me a few times, and then leaps up straight into my lap. Purring and meowing very loudly, with her tail standing right up, she nuzzles and rubs herself all over me while her beautiful eyes are firmly fixed on mine. She must have recognised my scent! I knew that she would always be my faithful cat. Being reunited with Chloe makes me burst into tears all over again.

CHAPTER THIRTY-ONE

Reunions

I'm woken by bright light piercing my eyelids. I throw my arm across my face to shield my eyes, and mentally swear at my selfish brother for turning a light on even though he knows I'm asleep. Gradually I become aware of a strange, hot sensation on my face which makes me open my eyes and sit bolt upright with fear. As my eyes dart around the room, I remember in an instant that I'm not in my bed in London being rudely awoken by Tony, but in Sophia's bedroom in Cyprus with the sun coming through the window, flooding the room with light and caressing my face with its heat. I can see my cousin asleep in the bed next to me and feel choked up with emotion to be here. I've only been in Cyprus for twenty-four hours and can't seem to stop crying with the happiness of it all, but thankfully I'm also laughing, and singing, and jumping with joy.

'Iouliaaaaa! Phone!' Sophia yells from the other room

after breakfast. Then she hands me the receiver for the fifth time in an hour. 'Just hurry up and get ready will you? We have so much to do and no time to do it in.'

As soon as all our old friends found out that I was here and staying with Sophia, they've been calling non-stop to arrange to meet up. The school term is not finished for them yet, since they still have another month to go before the Greek Easter holidays, so weekends are the only time I can see them.

My cousin is already dressed and ready to go out, wearing one of the outfits she was allowed to keep from my mum's collection. My mum, who is staying with one of her sisters who lives across town, left all the clothes with us for Sophia and her sisters to choose from. We had the best time last night choosing and trying on all the clothes from London and deciding which ones they wanted to keep, although my uncle had a few things to say about them. He seems to think that everything is either too short, too low cut, or too bright for a nice girl who is still at school. He's just so behind the times, unlike my mum, who approves of all my clothes. He didn't dare say anything about what Sophia's older sister chose, but in his opinion nearly everything was unsuitable for Sophia. I couldn't believe it! My dad never says anything about my clothes and even if he did, my mum would put him right. I tell Sophia that I don't remember my uncle being this strict.

'Oh God! Don't you remember how impossible he is about everything?' she says.

Frankly, no, I just don't seem to remember any of this; he seemed fine last summer in London, but I guess as far as clothes went, Sophia probably wore what she always wore, and from his perspective that was fine.

The last time I was in a busy shopping centre with my cousin was on Oxford Street nearly a year ago, so walking arm in arm with her along the main street in Nicosia, I feel as if I'm in a kind of dream. Am I really in Cyprus? I pinch myself to make sure I'm awake and hug my cousin tight. It's wonderful! It's brilliant! I skip along in the sunshine and feel totally happy to be here.

But somehow things look different to me. Everything is so much smaller than I remember, and although the shops have everything that English shops have, it's on a much smaller scale and with less choice. The main shopping street is pedestrianised so we can walk in the middle of it without fear of being run over. I have got so used to fighting my way through London's busy pavements and seeing a thousand people and cars, red buses and black taxi cabs whizzing by in all directions, that this seems really quite tame in comparison.

The spring sun feels hot to me so I take off my jumper, exposing my naked arms. It's so nice not to be wearing any tights under my short denim skirt, but my skin has become so pale from the long grey winter in England. Everywhere we go people stare and smile and one boy walks across the street and offers me a flower.

'Why is everyone staring?' I ask Sophia, suddenly feeling self-conscious as we walk along eating our favourite ice cream from our favourite shop.

'They think you are a tourist because of the way you're dressed,' she says with a giggle, and points at a group of girls walking in front of us who are wearing coats and boots.

'But it's hot,' I protest, and of course immediately remember that it's only the beginning of spring. In Cyprus, it gets so hot in summer that the heat can burn holes in the pavements, so springtime still feels quite chilly when you live here. Suddenly I feel really stupid, and like a foreigner. Oh my God, I realise and blush. I'm like all those tourists we used to make fun of, because they'd start stripping the minute the sun comes out, no matter what season it is.

CHAPTER THIRTY-TWO

Catching Up

Wow! I feel like a celebrity! For the last three hours, while sitting at an outdoor café, I've had a stream of friends drop by, and although I haven't exactly been signing autographs, I'm starting to feel like I should be.

Maria and Anastasia, Eleni and Luca, Sylvia and Rita, even my old boyfriend, Marco – they've all turned up to see me . . . although, I have my suspicions some are here just to *look at* me and see if I've changed.

The noise coming from our table is phenomenal. Everyone is talking all at once as there is so much to say and catch up on. I ask them a million questions about what's happened since I left, and they in turn want to know all about England, about my friends, school, shopping, boys . . . and I don't know what to tell them and in what order. I keep thinking the waiter is going to tell us to shut up, but instead he keeps smiling and bringing us more coffees. Then I remember that this is Cyprus and everyone is noisy here. Noise is a part of the way of life and people shout at each other as a matter of course and not just when they are fighting.

As I watch my friends come and go, I notice how much they've changed too, and how much older they look in just a year and half. The girls look really grown up in their make-up and clothes and the boys look as old as my brother. There is a marked difference in their appearance to my friends in London, but I can't quite put my finger on it.

'You are so white, Ioulia!' Eleni suddenly exclaims, so loudly that everyone can hear. 'What happened to you?'

'Nothing *happened* to me, I just haven't been in the sun much,' I reply, thinking that she's being a bit rude. 'I've been in England, remember? It rains a lot there.' Although I notice that Eleni doesn't look particularly golden brown or sun-kissed herself, I bite my tongue as we have so much else to talk about. I find myself thinking that Linda would never be so tactless, and I wonder if perhaps some English mannerisms might have rubbed off on me after all?

'So, do English girls straighten their hair, or do they all have it curly like you?' Rita chirps, and reaches over to touch the ends of my hair, bringing to my attention that every single one of my friends – apart from Sophia – has identical, perfectly blow-dried, straight hair. 'I suppose the damp weather makes it frizzy,' she says, adding insult to injury.

'Do you normally have to use lots of products in it?' says

Maria, just to make me feel even worse about my hair.

Well! Now I really *am* offended. Can't they think of anything more interesting to talk about apart from the state of my hair or skin colour? I dart a look at Sophia, who's grinning at me because, as usual, she knows exactly what's going through my mind.

'Actually, girls in England usually have straight hair but they all wish they had curly hair like me, *they* like it!' I say, and immediately begin to regret it. I shouldn't have stooped to that level, no matter how irritated I've become with this superficial conversation. I look around at all my old friends and suddenly it becomes clear to me how this group of girls differs from my friends in London. Here everyone is groomed and polished down to their French-manicured fingernails, perfect make-up, glossy straightened hair, and matching shoes and handbags. They are all so stylish, but they all look like clones of each other.

In London everyone is individual and quirky. Sure, a lot of people on the street or Underground are a mess, but girls – and boys – who care about fashion have a real eye for dressing in a way that is their own and not copying their look straight out of a magazine. Take boys like Sam or Nima, for instance. They are so creative and their dress sense is really cool, and all my girl friends have their own special sense of style too, making it look easy and trendy. Everyone here looks like they've tried a little too hard – even the boys.

I suddenly feel shaken by my train of thought. I can't

believe I am sitting in my beloved Cyprus with all my dearest friends, who I have been dying to see for all this time, and I'm criticising them and comparing them to people in London. What's happened to me?

'For God's sake, Sophia, why are they all being so shallow and superficial?' I ask my cousin on the way home from the café. 'I can't believe how everyone's changed in a year and half. I really don't remember them being like that,' I add, with a heavy heart.

'It's not them, Ioulia *mou*, it's you!' Sophia replies.

'What do you mean by that?' I ask, horrified. 'You mean I've changed? How have I changed? *You* don't think I've changed, do you?'

'I think you are as wonderful as ever and I love you just the same, but you *have* changed, you've . . .'

'How?' I demand, not letting her finish.

'You are so much more mature than any of them. You've grown up since you went away.'

'So have you!' I say, butting in again. 'You're not like them!'

'Maybe not, but you've changed in a different way. You live in such a different world now, but we all still live here. You might think they've changed in the way they look, but they are exactly the same in the way they think. You've just forgotten what it was like before you left.'

'We didn't just talk about hair and make-up all the time,' I protest.

'Yes, we did – most of the time. You and I always talked

about other stuff too, but with the others it was always the same. Don't forget you live in London now, and this is a very small place. You've just moved on, Ioulia *mou*, you are . . . more . . . *sophisticated*, I think is the word.'

'You are too!' I protest again.

'It may be so, but I've got you, and I've been to London and met your friends and you tell me things. Your move to England and adjusting to a different culture has made you more grown up than most of us. Some of our friends haven't even travelled to another country yet. You *live* in another country now. You've seen a different way of life, and that changes a person.'

CHAPTER THIRTY-THREE

More Than One Way to Love

'And where have you two young ladies been?' My uncle says to us the minute we walk in through the front door of the house. He's standing in the hallway with knotted eyebrows and his arms folded across his chest. 'You are not in London now, and you can't just come and go as you please,' he says, looking at both of us but mainly me. I can't believe this. Surely my uncle must know London is more dangerous than Nicosia, and surely he must realise we were just having coffee with a bunch of friends in a small, peaceful town with no dangers lurking around every corner. Where the hell did he think we were?

'Sorry, Papa,' Sophia says quickly as I open my mouth to protest, and then she grabs me by the hand and drags me away.

'What's wrong with him?' I ask in amazement. 'And why the apology? We did nothing wrong.'

'No point arguing with him. Best to just walk away and he'll forget. Besides, we are going out again, remember?

No point antagonising him now.'

I'm speechless. Does he think we are babies? And what about respect for young adults? I thought my stupid brother was bad, but my uncle beats him hands down.

'How's he going to let us go out tonight if he's in such a bad mood?' I ask.

'I don't know, we'll just have to battle it out with him,' she says. 'He'll drop us off and probably wait outside till we're done. But who cares.' We start laughing and getting ready. Our cousin Christina has arranged a party for me this evening to see all the friends and cousins who didn't make it to the café. I haven't been to a party since Nima's New Year's Eve party and I can't wait. There is also a boy Sophia really, really likes and she is dying for me to meet him.

'I hope you approve,' she says excitedly, 'He's gorgeous and I know we are on the verge of getting together. I haven't kissed him yet, so tonight's the night! Oh . . . his lips look so kissable!'

My cousin Christina's house is fabulous. They have a swimming pool in their huge back garden which has been landscaped and planted with giant cacti and exotic flowers. There are also six lemon trees all in a row just behind the pool which have been decorated with fairy lights especially for the occasion. The place looks very Hollywood and glamorous. Unlike Ari's house which was illuminated to death, the lighting here is very tasteful and totally appropriate – plenty of light in the garden and round the pool and very moody and atmospheric in the house.

My uncle dropped us off, saying he'd be back soon, but we ignore him and run into the house to see who's arrived. All the cousins and my friends from school have come, as well as a bunch of slightly older boys who I've never met before – friends of Christina's brother, Tony, I guess. It looks like it's going to be a great party. Sophia is wearing another of the outfits my mum brought and she looks gorgeous and seductive as she points out the boy of her dreams.

Suddenly, to my horror, from the corner of my eye I catch an unexpected glimpse of my auntie talking to my mum – who is definitely *not* supposed to be here. I thought this was a strictly teenagers-only party. I haven't seen much of my mum since we arrived, so I have no idea what she is doing here. Seconds later, I see yet another aunt and uncle, then another aunt, and then another uncle! In fact, all of a sudden I realise the *entire* family – parents, grand-parents and their friends – are dotted about everywhere. What a disaster, I think, and I rush up to Christina to point out the unwelcome guests.

'What are they all doing here?' I ask.

'Please don't even speak about it or I shall burst into tears,' she says, then grabs my arm and squeezes it. 'I pleaded with them to leave us alone and I thought I'd convinced them, but at the last minute they changed their minds and decided to come.'

'*Why?*' I ask her in total amazement. 'This is terrible! Every single old person we know is here! What are they doing at our party?'

'Have a guess,' Christina says, looking like she might be on the verge of tears now.

'I have no idea.'

'My parents feel they should be giving you *and* your mum a welcome party and since you're only here for such a short time, tonight seemed a good opportunity. Can you believe it? Anyway, Ioulia *mou*, I know the real reason – they just don't trust us. They never like the idea of me having a party with just my friends. Every time I try, they always ruin it.'

'What do they think we are going to do? Have an orgy? Honestly, they are impossible!'

It's so unfair. What a bunch of spoilsports they all are. My mind flashes back to Nima's New Year's Eve party and it makes me realise how much more tolerant parents are in London. Parents in Cyprus are so distrustful. It wouldn't hurt them to give their kids a bit more freedom. I start looking for Sophia to break the tragic news and prepare her for the fact that there will be no snogging for her and Mr Sexy Lips tonight. In one part of the house the party is in full swing and everyone is having fun. There is a happy buzz filling the air. A bunch of kids are dancing in one of the rooms that the parents haven't yet infiltrated and I spot Sophia in deep, pre-snogging conversation with her love god. I can also see that this has the makings of a great party, apart from the fact that we will all soon be tragically subjected to the beady eyes of our elders.

'I don't want Ioulia influencing Sophia too much with her English ways.' I hear my uncle's muffled words from behind our bedroom wall later on that night as Sophia and I are getting ready for bed. 'And the way she's dressed, she attracts too much attention.'

It feels like a slap in the face. On the verge of tears, I turn to look at my cousin. 'What does he mean, my English ways?'

'He's unforgivable! Please, Ioulia *mou*, don't take any notice.'

'I don't know what's he talking about. What ways? I'm still me, aren't I? I haven't grown a tail and horns since I went to England.'

'Of course you are still you and I love you *and* your ways, and I'm counting on you influencing me all you can,' Sophia tells me, and gives me a big hug. 'It's what we were talking about before, about you being more grown up and speaking your mind and all that. You're bound to have been influenced a bit living in London, and it's a *good* thing too. He's just a stupid old dad, stuck in the last century and scared of change.'

Although I'm tired after the party, once I climb into bed I find it impossible to sleep. I lie there, wide awake, with my uncle's and Sophia's words echoing in my ears.

What my uncle said was really hurtful and, perhaps without meaning to, he has managed to make me feel like an outsider in a house I used to consider a second home. Although I'm upset, I'm also starting to think there must be some truth in what Sophia said today. While I toss and turn in bed, and Sophia lies there, sleeping soundly in the bed next to me, I find myself thinking about the people I've left behind in London. I'm in my country, which I love more than anything in the world, but I'm thinking of England, which I've been dying to get away from and where I thought I felt like an outsider. What is going on? What is happening to me?

I love being in Cyprus, I love the light and the sun, the trees and the sea, the mountains and the air. I love my grandfather and my faithful cat, my cousins and aunties and uncles – even the ones who are a pain – the streets, the houses, the food, the music . . . I love it all. But at the same time, in a strange way, I feel nostalgic for London. I don't miss the rain or the cold or the grey sky, but I miss the buzz of the traffic and the rush of excitement as I run down the escalator to the Tube, the incredible sense of freedom. And I miss my friends. I miss Linda and Anna and even stupid Stella – who I will definitely call up when I get back – and Nima, and the way a boy like Sam can make me feel. I even miss my unbearable brother, who, although he bugs me, doesn't interfere in my life.

How can this be? I think, as I lie in bed with my head buzzing. Is it possible that from now on I will feel both love *and* alienation in two countries? Will I eventually feel that I belong in one or both places, or will I belong nowhere at all? I suppose if I can love both of my parents equally and at the same time – or, more to the point, if I can have feelings for two boys at the same time, then it should be possible to love two places. Perhaps, I think, as I slowly start to drift off to sleep, the kind of love for each place or for each person would be different, but it would be love nevertheless . . .

As the early morning sun pours into the room, waking me up again with its soft, warm caress, I turn to see if Sophia is awake and see her leaning on her elbow and smiling sweetly at me.

'Good morning, Ioulia *mou*, are you OK?'

'Fine. You?'

'I've been worrying about what my dad said last night. I don't want you to be upset by it. I'm really sorry.'

'No, Sophia *mou*, it's fine,' I say, overflowing with love for my wonderful cousin, and immediately I want to share my thoughts from last night with her. 'I couldn't sleep for hours and I've been thinking about everything and I've decided that you are so right. Things *have* changed, and the changes are good. I can't undo what's happened to me and if I'm different now, then that's how it is. In a way I'm lucky, because from now on I will always have you and Cyprus, but there will also be London too.'

If you would like more information about
books available from Piccadilly Press
and how to order them, please visit
our website at:

www.piccadillypress.co.uk